THE
PIPER

THE PIPER

DANNY WESTON

ANDERSEN PRESS • LONDON

First published in 2014 by
Andersen Press Limited
20 Vauxhall Bridge Road
London SW1V 2SA
www.andersenpress.co.uk

2 4 6 8 10 9 7 5 3 1

British Library Cataloguing in Publication Data available.

ISBN 978 1 78344 051 1

Printed and bound in Great Britain by
CPI Group (UK) Ltd, Croydon CR0 4YY

For Bob and Brenda Singfield

PART ONE
OVERTURE

PROLOGUE

7TH SEPTEMBER 1874

It's the music that wakes Alison. She opens her eyes and is instantly alert, with only one thought in her mind: They are in the garden again.

She turns her head to look towards the window. There's a soft wash of moonlight filtering in, picking out the faces of the dolls that sit in a row on the window seat, watching her. Then the voice speaks, a soft, entreating whisper.

Tillie's voice.

Alison! Get out of bed. Go and look!

It must be past midnight, a time when she should be fast asleep, but how *can* she sleep when the music is still playing, that sweet, lilting refrain? High-pitched and reedy, it sounds to her like a flute or a recorder. She can't help herself. She pushes aside the covers and climbs out of bed, then pads softly across the bare floorboards to the window.

Outside, the garden is wreathed in a thick grey mist that floats a foot or so above the grass. At first, the garden appears to be empty and she feels a jolt of disappointment spill through her. But then she sees them, dancing towards her along the avenue of trees at the top of the lawn, their jerky figures twirling and swaying in time to the music. It's the same two girls she saw the night before, she's sure of that, their faces pale in the moonlight, their long unkempt hair hanging into their eyes. Now they seem to become aware of her and one of them lifts a hand to beckon, just as she always does. Alison knows she wants her to join in the dance and she is tempted. So tempted. That's when Tillie's voice pipes up again.

Why not go out there? Just once? You know you'd love to.

'I shouldn't,' she whispers. 'It's late.'

But the music. Listen! Doesn't it call to you? Wouldn't you love to dance with the other children? Just this one time?

And she has to admit that she would. She is itching to do it, has been ever since she first started hearing that maddening tune a week ago – faint and distant at first, but getting closer every night. And besides, what would be the harm? Who would even know? She turns away from the window and heads for the door. She opens it as silently as she can, but it gives a maddening creak as it swings back, making a noise that seems to reverberate throughout the house. She stands for a moment, breathing heavily, listening, ready to run back to bed if she hears the sound of somebody coming to investigate...but no, there's just a deep rhythmic snore coming from the room to her left and the ticking of the old grandfather clock down in the drawing room. She steals out onto the landing, placing her feet with care on the ancient wooden boards. She stands there for a moment, needing to be sure she won't be discovered out of bed. Then she goes down the stairs.

In a matter of moments, she is at the front door of the house. She slides back the big bolts, wincing at the scraping of rusty metal on metal. Then she pushes the door open and, taking a deep breath, she steps outside. It's a warm summer's night and a full moon hangs in the sky – bigger, rounder than she's ever seen it before. Her nostrils savour the tang of freshly mown grass. Out here, the music is so sweet, so compelling, it is irresistible. She looks across the mist-shrouded lawn and there are the girls, dancing together and still beckoning to her to join them. Not for the first time, she wonders who they are, what has brought them out here to dance in the dead of night. She starts to walk towards them and, as she does, she throws a look over her shoulder at the house. Everything is in darkness. Nobody knows she's out here...

But she can't think about that now, she is intent on joining the other girls. Even as she runs towards them, she sees that they're moving away from her, heading back towards the avenue of trees at the top of the lawn. Far off, she thinks she glimpses another figure, a man, and she starts to think that the music is somehow emanating from him. But he too is moving away, striding purposefully towards the gates that lead to the marsh.

'Wait for me!' she whispers, but the girls pay her no heed, they keep dancing away through the mist as though intent on following the man, as though he is somehow drawing them like moths to a flame. Alison goes after them, determined to catch up, but at the same time aware that she is moving further and further away from home. She tries telling herself that she should turn back, but the music seems to fill her head now, it too is urging her to follow. And she knows she has to catch up with the girls somehow. She only wants that one quick dance.

In what seems like moments, they are out of the grounds and moving across the flat expanse of land beyond.

She cannot see the grass beneath its cover of mist, but she can feel the lush summer growth flattening under the soles of her feet. She is beginning to feel annoyed. Every time she thinks she's close to catching up with the girls, they dance away again, keeping themselves tantalisingly just out of her reach. If she falls too far behind, thinking of giving up the chase, they pause to summon her onwards again.

She has no idea how long she's been following them or how much ground she's covered, but up ahead is the line of trees that follows the banks of the Military Canal. The two girls move to the edge of the water and then they wait there. They begin to sway and whirl in the shadows of the trees, as though abandoning themselves completely to the music. Now they are beckoning to Alison to join them, and this time nobody is moving away from her. This time they are waiting. Waiting for her to join them.

Delighted, she quickens her step. She reaches the girls and begins to dance with them, copying their strange, jerky steps, flinging out her arms and stamping her feet, her whole body thrilling to the swooping, soaring sound of the flute. For a moment, she is transported. She has never known such joy, such pleasure.

And then, quite abruptly, the music stops.

She comes to her senses. She finds herself standing with two ragged strangers and suddenly, horribly, it comes to her how far from home she is, how very vulnerable. She looks at the girls and begins to see them in more detail. The first of them turns to stare at her and she sees that the girl's face is beyond pale. Her skin is the colour of bleached parchment and her mouth hangs open, wide, wider than she would have thought possible. A thread of drool dangles from her bottom lip. She takes a lurching step towards Alison. As Alison backs away she collides with the other girl standing just behind her. An overpowering stench fills her nostrils and, when she turns, she gasps in horror – the girl has no eyes and the empty sockets of her skull are writhing with clusters of glistening, grey worms.

She gasps again, pulls away and backs instinctively towards the bank of the canal, aware as she does so that the girls are walking slowly after her. She catches fleeting images of things she does not want to see – rotting flesh, lengths of exposed bone... and then she is standing by the canal bank, her bare feet teetering on the very edge, staring frantically this way and that. She wants to scream, but can find no sounds within her. She wants to run, but her legs seem to have lost the power to do anything more than hold her upright. She knows how to swim and, if she has to, she will fling herself into the water and power her way to the far bank.

Then she becomes aware of a man, standing a short distance away, watching in silence. She has an impression of a mouldering uniform: grimy epaulettes, rotting gold braid, mildewed leather boots. Some last desperate instinct tells her to speak to him, that he alone has the power to help her.

'Please,' she whispers. Just the one word. It's all she can manage.

But he simply lifts a long white pipe to his lips and begins to play again, that same, mournful tune.

Then a pair of cold wet hands clamp tightly around her ankles. She looks down in mute shock to see that the hands have risen up out of the water behind her. They pull back hard and she has time for one, short scream, before she flops down hard onto her face, the impact driving the breath out of her lungs. She digs her fingers into the soft earth of the canal bank and tries desperately to hang on, but the force pulling her is too powerful to resist for long. Her fingernails tear and she slides backwards into the water. Then she's under the surface, the oily olive green water is in her mouth and nostrils and she is dimly aware of more hands reaching up to her, clinging tightly onto her arms and legs as they take her down into the icy weed-choked darkness...

CHAPTER ONE

NOW

Helen turns her bicycle off the main road into the car park of the Summer View Care Home. She tries not to laugh at the irony of the name. It's late May, almost June, but it might as well be November; it's a cold, blustery day with dark clouds choking the sky and the threat of rain in the air.

It's not the best day for a bike ride, but with Mum out of the country on business and Dad down with one of his famous migraines, Helen's the only one capable of visiting Grandad Peter on his eighty-eighth birthday. Dad was supposed to be driving the two of them here this afternoon, but he claims to be feeling too ill. Helen's determined that somebody should visit her grandad. She's sure he has a soft spot for her, even if he isn't always good at showing it.

She chains her bike to some railings then heads towards the entrance, nodding to Eileen, the plump, friendly receptionist in the foyer.

'All on your own today?' asks Eileen, looking rather disapproving. She clearly doesn't think that a fourteen-year-old has any right to be out on her own.

'Dad's not feeling too good,' says Helen, by way of explanation.

'Very well, my dear. You know the way.'

Helen smiles and heads across the foyer, her feet making no sound on the thick pile carpet. Off the main corridor is Grandad Peter's door. She raps gently on it.

'Come in.' He manages to make the two words sound weary, and even Helen's spirits sink a little. This clearly isn't going to be much fun. She takes a deep breath and steps into the room, which is filled with that 'old person' smell – equal parts vegetable soup and Vick's VapoRub. There are a couple of rather pathetic-looking red balloons floating in one corner of the room, the nursing staff's attempt to add a sense of occasion, Helen supposes, but it has failed dismally. The room is about as jolly as a funeral.

Grandad Peter is sitting in his armchair in front of the window, gazing out at the well-tended gardens. He doesn't even turn his head to see who's come to visit him and Helen feels a twinge of irritation. Strange old Grandad Peter, with his thin face and his haunted eyes and his odd, detached *manner. Helen likes the old man, she really does, but he doesn't make it easy. Perhaps it's because she senses a terrible sadness in him, as though something happened to him back in the day and he's never quite managed to get out from under its shadow.*

She's never understood why he and Dad don't seem to get along, the two of them so distant, hardly ever speaking to each other. Grandad Peter's wife, Emily, died more than a year ago, so Helen knows she needs to make a special effort with him because he must be so lonely. She unhooks the rucksack and takes out the slightly battered cake in its bright blue box.

'Happy birthday!'

He looks at her for a moment, his cold blue eyes seeming to study her, evaluate her. She realises that she hasn't really ever spent time with Grandad Peter on her own before. He's never shown her much affection, not like most of her friends' grandparents, but she's always felt that deep down he does care about her. She finds herself wondering what happened to him to make him like this – so cold, so distant. God knows how Grandma put up with him for all those years. After a few moments, he nods and gestures to the little table at his side. 'Put it there,' he says. 'I'm not hungry now.'

Helen feels another stab of irritation. She's spent her own pocket money on this, would it kill him to try a taste of it? But she says nothing. She sets the cake down and hands him the card instead. 'This is from all of us,' she lies.

'Thanks. You really shouldn't have bothered.'

'Of course we should!' She takes off her jacket and drapes it over the back of a spare chair. 'It's a big day, Grandad. Your eighty-eighth birthday.'

His eyes widen slightly, as though he's somehow surprised to hear this news. She watches as he tears open the envelope, pulls out the card and studies it dutifully. It depicts a smiling cartoon grandad, wearing a flat cap and tartan slippers, reclining in a chair with a huge tankard of beer in one hand and the words WORLD'S BEST GRANDAD printed in big red letters across the top. Helen can't help but think how unlike the old man the cartoon is. He rarely smiles and, as far as she's aware, he's a lifelong teetotaller, but there wasn't much to choose from. It was either this or cards featuring golf, racing cars or football, none of which he's the least bit interested in. She watches as he reads the brief message she's scrawled inside.

'Happy birthday, Grandad!' she tries again. She's signed her own name and faked Mum and Dad's signatures, trying

to vary the handwriting for each of them. She doubts that he's fooled for an instant. He closes the card and sets it down beside the cake. 'That was nice of you,' he says. 'Very nice.' A long pause. 'So, it's just you then?'

'Yes.' Helen tries not to feel resentful as she settles into the rocking chair beside him. What's so bad about her? At least she's better than nobody. 'Mum's in Oslo for that conference thing? I spoke to her on the phone yesterday. She, er...asked me to pass on her best wishes to you. Says we'll take you out for a meal when she gets back.'

'Oslo?' He looks baffled. 'What on earth is she doing in Oslo?'

'Some kind of lecture at the university. Something to do with the environment?' She shrugs her shoulders. Mum's work has always been pretty much a mystery to her. 'She says they've put her in a nice hotel.'

Peter nods. 'She's a busy lady,' he said. 'And...Tony?'

'Feeling poorly. Another migraine. He sends his love.'

This is a lie. When she'd spoken to Dad just before she left the house, he'd said nothing about his father's birthday, not until she'd brought it up. He'd been lying on the sofa at the time, with a wet flannel on his forehead. Dad's migraines are legendary, though he only ever seems to go down with

15

one whenever there's something he doesn't want to do. Like visiting his father.

'Dad, we're supposed to go and visit Grandad Peter,' she'd pleaded with him. 'You know, for his birthday and everything? You promised you'd take me.'

'I know I did, love, but I'm feeling lousy.'

'Well, then I'll just have to go by myself, won't I? On the bike.'

He'd pulled a face at this. 'You know I don't like you going on those busy roads all by yourself,' he'd said.

'So come with me.'

'I can't, love, really. Maybe we'll go one night in the week.'

'But his birthday's today!'

'I know, but...' He gestured at the flannel. 'I wouldn't be very good company, I'm afraid. My head's pounding and my vision... I wouldn't be safe to drive.'

'All right, then I'm going without you.'

'Helen, wait a minute...'

But that was that. She'd stormed out of the house, got her bike from the garage and cycled the three miles to the care home. It was a Sunday and the roads were pretty quiet anyway.

Now Helen feels she has to make excuses. She looks at Grandad Peter and rolls her eyes. 'Poor Dad. He was completely out of it when I left.'

'He does suffer with those migraines,' admits Grandad Peter. 'Always has, even when he was a little boy.'

'So I thought I'd just … you know, come over myself.'

'How did you get here?'

'On the bike.'

He scowls. 'You need to be careful,' he tells her. 'The roads are full of maniacs, these days. Complete and utter headcases.'

'Hmm.' Helen takes this with a large pinch of salt. She knows for a fact that the old man has never learned to drive. 'Dad said it was OK,' she tells him.

Another lie.

'So … how's school?' he asks her.

'Oh, not so bad.' She smiles. 'Lots of homework. We've got a new history teacher, Miss Jacobs. She's a bit of a frump, but I quite like her. And I'm looking forward to going away in September.'

'Going away?'

'Yes, there's a school trip. Mum said I could put my name down for it.'

'Anywhere interesting?'

'I'm not sure. I was going to ask you, actually. It's somewhere you've been before, I think.'

That's enough to get his attention. He turns his head to look at her.

'Whatever do you mean?' he murmurs.

'Well, didn't you say once that you went there when you were little? To Romney Marsh.'

Something strange happens to Grandad Peter's face. It's as though he's been asleep and, suddenly, somebody has snapped a switch to wake him up. He sits bolt upright in his chair and stares at her.

'You're…going to Romney Marsh?'

'Yes. To an outward-bound centre. We're going to be…'

But he's shaking his head from side to side. 'No,' he says. 'No, no, no, you can't go. I absolutely forbid it!'

Helen feels like laughing at this, but the expression on his face hasn't got anything to do with laughter. He looks scared. She stares at him, puzzled by his sudden animation. 'What's wrong?' she asks him. 'You've gone all pale.' She starts to get up from the rocking chair, worried about him. 'Perhaps I'd better get somebody,' she says, but he grabs her arm, pulls her back down into a sitting position.

She is momentarily shocked by the strength in those skinny arms.

'Where?' he demands to know. 'Where exactly are you going?'

'I already told you. Romney Marsh.'

'Yes, but...the name. The exact name of the place!'

'I don't know...' Helen struggles to remember. She has no idea what's wrong with him, she's never seen him like this before. 'Somewhere near Rye, I think...It's one of those activity holidays. There's all kinds of things to do. You know, hiking, boating...'

'Boating?' Now he looks really agitated. 'Listen to me, Helen, you...you can't go there. It's...it's not safe.'

She laughs, a tad hysterically. His evident terror is starting to get to her.

'It's...OK,' she assures him. 'They have these trained instructors and everything. It'd be more dangerous crossing the road.'

'You don't know!' he roars, and the anger in his voice almost rocks her back in her seat. 'You silly girl! I was there. I was on the Marsh in the war, me and Daisy. We were just children. We saw everything. Everything. We saw too much.'

Daisy? Who's Daisy? Helen has never heard him mention the name before. 'Look,' she says. 'I can see that you're worried, but…I'm a big girl now. I'm nearly fifteen. And it's not as if I'll be on my own. The whole class is going and…' *Her voice trails away when she realises that he isn't listening to her. His eyes have a faraway look in them. He starts to talk, his voice soft and low, but gaining in power as he goes on.*

'I went there in September, 1939,' *he murmurs.* 'It was a strange time. Everyone knew that war was coming and they thought the big cities would be bombed within days…'

Helen stares at him. She realises he's talking about something he's never spoken of before, at least never to her, something that happened to him long ago.

'Somebody came up with the bright idea of sending thousands of us children out to the countryside, where they thought we'd be safe.' *He laughs, a bitter laugh.* 'I expect they meant well. They couldn't have known. How could they? So they packed us up and sent us all away to different places across the country. It was a government initiative, this evacuation. They called it…Operation Pied Piper…'

CHAPTER TWO

FRIDAY 1ST SEPTEMBER 1939

The rhythmic rattle of the old train should have been enough to lull Peter to sleep but there were too many thoughts careering around in his head to allow for that. Daisy had finally stopped crying a few miles back and she was now fast asleep with her head on his shoulder.

He was worried about Daisy. Leaving his parents in London had been bad enough for him, and he was thirteen, nearly grown up. Daisy was only seven and being torn away from Mum had been the worst thing that had ever happened to her. Mum had told Peter, the night before they'd left home, that he would have to be responsible for Daisy now. With Dad called up and Mum working shifts at the Ford factory, it was up to him to keep his sister safe until the war was over and they could come home again.

They had been up at six o'clock that morning and Mum had accompanied them to St Bartholomew's, which was being used as an assembly point for all the schools in the area. From there, hundreds of children and their parents had marched in a column to a place where specially chartered buses were waiting to take them to Waterloo Station. A designated teacher walked at the head of each group. The children chatted excitedly amongst themselves, the boys trying to outdo each other in guessing how far they might be expected to travel. Arthur Hayes, whose father was a bank manager, claimed that he'd had a tip-off that they would all end up in Australia, but Mr Griffiths, Peter's teacher, told Arthur in no uncertain terms to pipe down and stop talking nonsense. Peter told himself that wherever they were bound, it was going to be exciting, because most of the children had never been out of London in their entire lives and none had spent time away from their parents. He looked up at his mother, who was walking hand-in-hand with Daisy beside him. Mum looked pale and stern and the red rings around her eyes betrayed the fact that she'd been crying recently.

They piled aboard the buses and set off for the station. When they arrived at Waterloo, they found a scene of complete chaos waiting for them. Hundreds and hundreds of children and their teachers were milling around on the crowded platforms, shouting at each other and brandishing sheets of printed paper. Train whistles shrieked and engines belched clouds of steam, adding to the confusion. Trains came and went, with people fighting to get onto them. Teachers traded insults with each other and some sets of parents even came close to exchanging punches. It was gone midday by the time St Bartholomew's were finally allocated a train and they hurried to their designated platform with no idea of where they were going or when they might get there.

Mum ignored the advice of the wardens, who told her to turn her back on the children as they walked away to make it 'easier on herself'. No, she hugged them and kissed them and burst into frantic tears as they pulled themselves out of her arms and clambered aboard the train.

'Don't forget,' she called to Peter as it rumbled out of the station. 'Whatever happens, look after your sister!'

After the noise and confusion of the station, the journey itself had come as a blessed relief – but as the train clattered onwards, with no sign of arriving anywhere, the novelty soon wore off. Peter looked out of the window and saw wide expanses of green fields and hedgerows stretched out in the September sunshine, so unlike anything he'd known back in Dagenham. It was hard to believe that a war was coming, but Neville Chamberlain had been on the radio only the other night, saying there was no avoiding it now. And yet, with everything so warm and sun-dappled and peaceful, it seemed unlikely that anything bad was ever going to happen.

Peter looked around the packed compartment to see other children, some he knew well, some he barely knew, slumped into the seats all around him, every one of them with a big brown label attached to his or her coat, stating their name, address and school. Their suitcases and gas masks were piled up on the luggage racks above them. They had begun the journey by singing popular songs to try and keep up their spirits, but as the time passed, the energy had drained out of them and now most of the children were fast asleep as they clattered through the countryside, to some unknown destination. To make matters worse, every so often the train would come to a halt and stand still for ages with no explanation given, before finally setting off again.

Daisy stirred and looked resentfully up at Peter, her blue eyes rimmed red from crying. 'Are we nearly there yet?' It was the sixth time she'd asked him. Her blonde curls were all in a tangle and her tiny body seemed swamped in the heavy overcoat she was wearing.

He could only shrug his shoulders. 'It shouldn't be too much longer,' he told her, but he had no idea if this were true.

'I miss Mummy.' Two large tears swelled in her eyes and trickled down her pale cheeks.

Peter knew how she felt, but he couldn't allow himself to admit it to her. Deep down inside, he was scared too. It was the first time in his life he'd been away from his parents for more than an hour or so. 'Think of it as an adventure,' he told Daisy.

She sniffed and looked up at him unconvinced.

'There'll be trees and fields to play in. Animals, I shouldn't wonder.' He warmed to the theme, knowing how she spent so much time looking wistfully at pictures of animals in books. 'Sheep...cows...maybe even deer.'

'You think so?'

'Of course. It's the countryside, isn't it? That's what they have out here. Everyone knows that. Look!' He pointed to the window and Daisy turned her head to see. Sure enough, the field they were passing was dotted with scores of white, woolly shapes.

'Sheep!' she exclaimed, as though she thought he wouldn't know what they were. He had to admit to himself that he couldn't remember ever having seen one before in the flesh. He'd been born and raised in the grey, smoky streets of Dagenham, and the few holidays the family had enjoyed had always been spent at the seaside, at Southend, where the only animals to be seen were seagulls and donkeys. For a moment, Daisy forgot the situation. She moved closer to the window for a better view and began to count the sheep as they passed by. She'd got as far as nineteen, when she stopped suddenly. Peter saw that in the field they were passing, a small white shape was lying slumped in the grass. A lamb. Around it fluttered dozens of black ragged birds, their beaks pecking frantically at the creature's head. Even at this distance, Peter could see the two empty black sockets where the lamb's eyes used to be. A few yards away, a sheep, probably the lamb's mother, looked on helplessly.

Daisy turned away from the window with a gasp of revulsion and Peter put his arm around her. 'It'll be all right,' he tried to assure her, but he knew how hollow that must sound. Her little shoulders slumped and she looked up at him, her bottom lip trembling. He could see she was close to crying again.

'How long,' she asked him, 'before we can go home?'

Peter sighed. 'Nobody really knows,' he admitted. 'But

Dad told me he reckons he could be home by Christmas.'
He didn't mention that Mum had added, in a grim voice,
that this is exactly what they'd said in the last war, or the
way Dad shot her a fierce look, as though warning her not
to say any more.

Peter's mind went back to last Christmas. It had been the
best ever. Dad had managed to get two whole days off work
and they'd had sticky dates to eat, some tangerines and even
a banana each! Peter had been given a Dinky Toy, a tiny
replica of a Rolls Royce, while Daisy had received a little
black-faced doll, whom she called Eva and went everywhere
with her. Even now, Eva was nestled safely in Daisy's case
along with her clothes, pyjamas and toothbrush.

'What if it's not over?' Daisy asked sulkily. 'What if it's
never over and we never see Mummy and Daddy again?'

'Don't be daft,' he told her. 'Of course it's going to be over.
No war lasts for ever. One side wins and the others have to
go back to where they belong.'

'But what if *we* lose?'

Peter didn't have an answer for that. He was relieved
when the train began to slow down and, with a great
screeching of brakes, it finally pulled into a station. After a
few minutes, they saw Mr Griffiths out on the platform,

walking along the length of the train and beckoning to everyone, shouting that it was time to get off. Peter stood up and slid down the window so he could hear better. Mr Griffiths was telling everyone to gather up their bags, cases and gas masks and to prepare themselves for a long walk.

Nobody argued. Nobody asked questions. The world had changed and there seemed to be nothing for it but to do whatever they were told.

CHAPTER THREE

The station was called Rye. Peter thought it was an odd name and it brought to mind an old song he'd heard at school, something about 'comin' through the rye'. He had a vague idea that rye was another word for corn and the song had always brought to mind visions of great fields of the stuff, swaying in the wind, but for the moment at least there was only a small country station with a couple of platforms. The children were herded off the train and told to form themselves up in a neat line. Then a woman stepped out of the waiting room, a tall thin woman dressed in a long khaki raincoat and wearing a beret. Mr Griffiths announced that she was Miss Halshaw, the Billeting Officer for this area, who'd been sent to make sure that everyone ended up in the right place. He told the children to follow her and then placed himself at the end of the line to watch out for any stragglers.

They marched out of the station and onto a busy road, then were led through Rye itself, a strange, old-fashioned town with narrow winding streets and white-painted cottages. The place had the fresh tangy smell of the sea, which reminded Peter of the family's occasional trips to Southend, but he couldn't actually see any water from here. There were seagulls flying overhead, though, screeching dementedly at the new arrivals as though telling them to get back to where they came from. Arthur Hayes was coming in for quite a bit of leg-pulling as some of the other boys pointed out that wherever they were, it wasn't Australia.

As he walked, Peter was aware of passers-by staring at the line of children, as though wondering what they were doing here. Hadn't anybody told them to expect the evacuees? He wasn't sure how far they walked, but it must have been a good thirty minutes before Miss Halshaw announced that they had reached their destination, a big wooden hut on the outskirts of the town. As they were shepherded in through the entrance, Peter noticed a sign beside the entrance, which announced that this place was a Friends' Meeting House.

Inside, there didn't seem to be anything in the least bit friendly about it. It was a scene of total chaos, every bit as crowded as the station had been, back in London. Miss

Halshaw pushed her way through the hustle and bustle, waving sheets of paper and talking to anybody who would listen to her. Meanwhile, women from the Women's Voluntary Service moved along the line of new arrivals, handing out brown paper bags. Peter looked in his and saw that it contained a tin of bully beef, a small packet of digestive biscuits, a stamped postcard (which he was told he should fill in and send home when he had 'landed somewhere') and best of all, a Kit Kat. He and Daisy wasted no time and unwrapped and ate theirs as they stood there, then started right in on the biscuits. After eating nothing since the lunch that Mum had packed for them, they were ravenous.

'This is daft,' Peter heard Arthur Hayes telling Roy Walters. 'When I get home, I'll tell my dad all about this and he'll send them a letter they'll never forget.'

'That'll scare 'em,' muttered Roy.

After a little while, Miss Halshaw reappeared, looking rather harassed. She told the children to climb up onto the stage at the end of the room and form a row in front of the curtains at the back, so they could be claimed by people standing in the crowd. As he moved past, Peter heard Mr Griffiths saying heatedly to Miss Halshaw, 'We were told that *every* child would have an appointed host. This is like a cattle auction.'

Miss Halshaw shook her head. 'It's more complicated than we'd hoped. Many of the people who originally agreed to take children have since been assigned others. I'm afraid this is really the only way we can do it.'

'It's most irregular! I don't see how...' The rest of Mr Griffiths' words were lost to Peter as somebody pushed him towards the stage. He kept a firm grip on Daisy's hand as they climbed the few steps. Then they looked down to see that rows of people were staring at them with interest, as though they *were* at an auction or something, just as Mr Griffiths had said. There was an uncomfortable silence, before a man in a flat cap and an overcoat pointed to Mark Watkins, a tall, dark-haired boy, and said, 'I'll take him.'

And so it began. One by one, the children were chosen. They had little option but to go obediently down the steps to their new hosts before having their details written down by Miss Halshaw. Peter held onto Daisy's hand, wanting to ensure that everybody understood the two of them came as a package. Children all around them were being picked. Peter noticed that the youngest children went first and some of the bigger, older boys, whom he supposed would probably make good farm workers. But it was the girls who seemed to be most in demand and one by one, they were beckoned down from the stage and taken away. Pretty soon there were only a few children left on the stage and Daisy was easily the youngest of them.

Then Peter noticed a woman pushing her way impatiently through the crowd, a tall but heavy-set woman in a long grey raincoat. She had a pale face and a hooked nose that was made all the more noticeable by a large black mole on one side of it. Her black hair was tied back in a tight bun and she had piercing dark eyes, set beneath thick eyebrows that met in the middle of her forehead. She looked grim and rather forbidding. She scanned the row of children intently and then her gaze settled on Daisy, as though interested in her.

Peter looked hopefully around, wondering if somebody might be prepared to take the pair of them, but was met only by blank stares. Then the hook-nosed woman raised a hand and pointed at Daisy. 'You, girl. How old are you?' she asked, in a loud, oddly accented voice.

Daisy replied, her voice faint. 'I'm s...seven, miss,' she said.

The woman nodded, as if this was exactly what she'd wanted to hear. 'I'll 'ave that one,' she announced, looking at Miss Halshaw and pointing at Daisy again, just to be sure there was no confusion. Daisy made a move to obey her, but Peter hung on tight.

'No!' he said, and a shocked silence fell over the room. Peter looked desperately at Miss Halshaw. 'We have to stay together. I promised my mum.'

Miss Halshaw looked annoyed, as though this was an unnecessary complication. But then she seemed to consider for a moment and she shrugged her shoulders. She smiled at the woman. 'Could you not take the two of them?' she asked. 'There'll be an extra payment if you have the boy as well.'

The woman scowled. 'I was told to get a young 'un. A girl. That's all I know.'

Mrs Halshaw smiled distastefully. 'Does the age matter that much? As you can see, there are still several boys who—'

'It has to be a girl!' cried the woman and she sounded annoyed. She scanned the rows of children, as if suspecting that another girl, on her own, might be hidden somewhere in their ranks, but her gaze kept returning to Daisy.

Miss Halshaw looked at Peter. 'Are you sure you couldn't agree to be separated?' she said. 'Perhaps just for a little while, until we can make the proper arrangements? It makes things very difficult when there's two of you.'

'I don't care,' said Peter fiercely. 'I promised Mum.' As if to emphasise the point, Daisy hugged him closer, burying her face against his stomach.

Miss Halshaw turned back to the woman. 'Well, you can see they're set on this,' she said, almost apologetically. She turned to look at the rows of waiting people. 'Perhaps there's somebody else here who would be prepared to take *both* children?' she asked.

But before anybody could answer, the woman stepped urgently closer to the stage, as though afraid that somebody else might get Daisy. 'Both then,' she snapped. 'I'll take 'em both.' She beckoned impatiently to Peter. 'Step down 'ere,' she told him. 'You and your sister. Look lively, we 'aven't got all day.'

Peter frowned, but did as he was told. Daisy was looking fearfully at the woman as she climbed down off the stage. It was apparent that she didn't much like what she saw and Peter felt the same way about it. There was something in the woman's manner that spoke of a reluctance to be here, as though she had more important things to attend to, and the way she was so insistent on having Daisy felt a bit sinister.

But she made a clumsy attempt at jollity and stepped closer, baring her teeth in an unconvincing grin. 'Now then,' she said, 'we'll be great friends, won't we? What are your names?'

'I'm Peter. And this is Daisy.'

'Daisy! What a lovely name. You'll make a perfect companion for a young girl around your age.' She barely glanced at Peter. 'Now, we'll go and do the paperwork, shall we? I expect you two are anxious to get some home-cooked food inside ye.'

The woman stepped over to Mrs Halshaw and started to give her details.

Daisy looked up at Peter crossly. 'She talks funny,' she said.

'It's just an accent,' Peter assured her. 'Shush a minute.' He edged a little closer, enough to overhear that the woman's name was Mrs Beesley and that she was the housekeeper to a Mr Alfred Sheldon of Sheldon Grange. She answered Mrs Halshaw's questions brusquely as though she resented having to bother with such silly details.

Just at that moment, Mr Griffiths came over to speak to Peter and Daisy, crouching down so his face was level with theirs. 'It looks as though you two are fixed up, at least,' he said. He glanced around the busy room and shook his head. 'Only a few more to sort out and I can think about heading back myself,' he added. He smiled reassuringly. 'As soon as you get to your host home, ask for the address and mail the postcard to your parents. Then they'll be able to drop you a line, to see how you're getting on. You won't let me down now, will you?'

'No, sir,' said Peter. 'We'll remember.'

Mr Griffiths reached out and shook his hand, then gave Daisy a reassuring pat on the shoulder. 'I know it's difficult,' he murmured, 'but we all have to do our bit for the war effort.' He straightened up and headed back into the crowd.

Peter watched him go and, as he did, he got the strangest feeling that he would never see Mr Griffiths or his old school again. Then he started as a hand clamped down on his shoulder. He looked up into the stern features of Mrs Beesley.

'We're all set,' she said. 'Let's be on our way.'

CHAPTER FOUR

Peter had hoped there would be a motorcar waiting for them, but he was disappointed when Mrs Beesley directed them to a shabby-looking pony and cart, waiting on the road outside the hall. A huge, bearded man sat up in the seat, holding the reins. Despite the warmth of the day, he was wearing a thick tweed overcoat with the collar turned up and a filthy flat cap. He studied the two children as they approached and watched in silence as Mrs Beesley directed them to climb into the back of the cart and make themselves as comfortable as they could.

'Two of 'em?' he muttered, as she clambered heavily up beside him. 'Dunno what Mr Sheldon will have to say about that.'

She directed a withering glare at him. 'You let me worry about that,' she growled. 'If certain people had hurried 'emselves up, there might have been more choice. I had to take what I could get.'

'It's not *my* fault,' he told her. 'Bessie's not gettin' any younger and I've told Mr Sheldon, I don't know 'ow many times, her near hind fetlock needs lookin' at. There's summin' not quite right with it.'

'None of us is gettin' any younger,' said Mrs Beesley. 'And there'll be something not quite right with you if we don't get to the Grange by nightfall. We don't want to be out after dark, do we?' She gave him a meaningful look and he reacted instantly, slapping the reins against the pony's flanks and telling her to 'giddy up'.

The cart lurched forward and the driver urged Bessie into a brisk trot. They turned left off the street and followed a road which seemed to be leaving the outskirts of town and heading into open country. Sitting behind his hosts in the clattering, juddering cart, Peter studied the backs of their heads for a few moments, hoping that one of them might say something; but when after several minutes neither of them had bothered, he felt moved to break the silence. 'Is it far to where we're going?' he asked.

Mrs Beesley turned her head to look back at him, as though she'd forgotten that he was there. 'It's a good distance,' she admitted. 'But we'll be there in an hour or so.'

Peter heard a soft groan emerge from Daisy's lips at this news. They'd been on the move since early morning and were both desperate to sit still for a moment. 'And...what is this Grange place?' he asked.

'It's a farm,' said Mrs Beesley. 'I expect you two won't have much idea about farms, eh, what with coming from Lunnen and all?'

'Lunnen?' Peter frowned. 'Do you mean...London?'

Now the driver turned his head, an amused smile on his potato-like face. 'Cheeky young rip, ain'tcha?' he said. 'Aye, London is what she meant, right enough. I'm Adam, by the way.' He removed one huge calloused hand from the reins and shook Peter's hand warmly.

'I'm Peter. This is Daisy. And I didn't mean to sound cheeky, sir, I've just never heard it said like that before.'

'That's just my accent,' said Mrs Beesley. 'Everyone talks like this round these parts. You'll soon get used to it.'

'You'll get used to *all* our funny ways,' said Adam and he winked.

'Will there be animals on the farm?' asked Daisy hopefully.

Adam smiled. 'Aye, we've animals right enough. You fond of 'em, miss?'

Daisy nodded. 'I've got books with pictures of them,' she said.

This seemed to amuse Adam. 'Why, bless thee, pictures she says! We've got the real thing at the Grange, don't you worry about that. There's sheep mostly. Romney Marsh sheep, I expect you've 'eard of 'em. Them's famous all around the world, them is.'

'They're not famous in Dagenham,' Peter assured him. 'At least... I don't think they are.'

Adam guffawed, as if he'd made a joke. 'Not famous in Dagenham!' he repeated. 'Bless my soul. You two are a right pair of jokers, ain'tcha?'

Peter and Daisy looked at each other blankly. Peter hadn't meant to say anything funny and didn't think that he *had*, but he decided it would be best not to mention it. He looked out at the countryside into which they were heading, a bleak stretch of flat moorland, through which the dirt road cut straight as a knife. The sun was already quite low on the horizon and turning a dull shade of orange. There wasn't a single tree or hill in sight, with the result that you could see for miles over the scrubby-looking grass. Occasionally, a channel of sluggish grey water meandered through the land and, here and there, they passed the occasional lake, but there was not much else of note. Peter wondered why none of the other children seemed to be heading in this direction. He suddenly got the strangest feeling: it felt as though he and the other occupants of the cart were the last people left in the world. Then he became aware of the silence. Apart from the clattering of the wheels on the road, the clunking of Bessie's hooves, and the creaking of her leather harness, there was not another sound to be heard. They rode along in this way for some time. Then:

'Here comes trouble,' announced Adam quietly. Peter saw over Adam's shoulder that a figure was approaching from up ahead, too distant as yet to make out much detail.

Mrs Beesley turned in her seat and pointed to a folded blanket that lay in the bottom of the cart. 'We're going to play a little trick on someone,' she announced. 'Get down on the floor, pull that blanket over yourselves, and both of you keep nice and quiet.'

Peter looked at her. 'But why—?'

'Never mind, why,' snapped Mrs Beesley. 'Like I said, it's a trick. Come along now, cover yourselves up and not a sound from either one of you!'

Bemused, Peter did as he was told, even though the blanket had a rather unpleasant animal smell about it. He and Daisy crouched down on the uncomfortable wooden floor. After a while, the cart eased to a halt and Peter heard a man's voice calling up to the passengers. It sounded hearty and more refined than Adam's or Mrs Beesley's.

'Hello there! Been into Rye, have you?'

'That's right,' said Adam. 'We had a few provisions to pick up.'

'Lots of excitement in the town today, I understand. The evacuees.'

'So I 'eard,' said Mrs Beesley's voice. 'We only called to the general store for a few bits and pieces, didn't we, Adam?'

'Aye, that's right.'

'I'd have liked to have billeted a child myself, but I'm not really equipped for it. I can't cook anything more than a boiled egg and, as I'm sure you know, my housekeeper walked out on me after all that unpleasantness about the book.'

'Oh, you haven't found a replacement yet?' asked Mrs Beesley.

'Afraid not. Tried everywhere. I don't suppose you know anyone?'

'Nobody. Not round 'ere.'

'Shame really, would have been nice to have a bit of

company around the place. I should have thought Alfred could have taken someone though? He's plenty of room. And it would have been a nice companion for—'

'You'll 'ave to excuse us, Professor,' interrupted Mrs Beesley. 'Only, it's getting late and we wants to be back by nightfall.'

'Oh, you've a little while yet, surely? I just wanted to ask you if—'

But then Peter heard the crack of the whip, cutting the voice off in mid-sentence. The cart moved on again.

'See you later then!' called the man's voice from somewhere behind them. He sounded disappointed.

After a little while, Mrs Beesley announced that it was all right to come out from under the blanket.

'What was that all about?' asked Peter, brushing his hair out of his eyes. 'And why did you say you hadn't seen us?'

'I told you. We was playing a trick. That fellow back there, he's a right old busybody. Always sticking his nose into other folks' business, he is. If he knew you two were staying with us, it'd soon be the talk of the town.'

'Folks in these parts likes to keep 'emselves to 'emselves,' said Adam. 'That's just the way we are.'

They rode along for some distance in silence. Peter felt moved to say something else, if only to hear the reassuring sound of his own voice.

'We have a postcard,' he announced, and the two adults turned their heads to look at him again. 'We're to fill it in with your address and send it off as soon as possible, so our mum can write to us.'

Mrs Beesley considered this information for a moment, then made that forced attempt at a smile. 'Goodness me, what's your 'urry?' she asked him. 'We're not even there yet. There'll be plenty of time for all that, once we've got you settled. I've a room already picked out for you,' she told Daisy. She glanced at Peter. 'And I expect we'll find one for you,' she added.

'Can't we stay together?' asked Daisy, sounding apprehensive.

'A big girl like you? Oh, don't be silly! It's time you had your own room. Mr Sheldon is the most successful farmer on the Marsh and the Grange is a great big place. So it would be silly to throw you in together, wouldn't it?'

'The ... Marsh?' asked Peter.

'Yes. Romney Marsh, of course. That's where the Grange is. Did nobody tell you where you'd be goin'?'

'Nobody told us anything,' said Peter.

'Well, that's where we're 'eaded, right enough,' said Adam. 'Romney Marsh, the biggest wilderness on God's earth. Lived 'ere all me life, I 'ave. I know the place like the back of me 'and.' He seemed to think for a moment. 'If you two should ever chance to be alone out here, you watch out for the canals,' he said.

'The canals?' Peter looked around but he couldn't see any water.

'Oh aye. They're out there, right enough, and sometimes you don't see 'em until you're right next to 'em. They can be dangerous. The water's dark and there's thick, clingin' weeds. Why, I remember once—'

'Let's have less of the chat,' Mrs Beesley interrupted him. 'And can't you get this 'orse moving faster?'

'I already told you,' said Adam. 'Her fetlock…'

'Never mind about her blessed fetlock! Use the goad if you have to.' She indicated a long leather whip that was standing in a container at Adam's side.

'It'll be all right,' Adam assured her. 'We'll be there in time.'

'We'd better be.' Peter noticed how Mrs Beesley kept looking towards the western horizon, where the sun was rapidly turning the clouds crimson.

As they moved on, he spotted a tiny stone building to his right. The place had once had a roof but that had fallen in and the remains of a stubby chimney stuck up at one end. It looked far too small for anybody to have actually lived in. 'What's that?' he asked, pointing.

Adam followed his gaze. 'That? It's an old sheep 'ouse,' he said.

'The sheep live in houses?' asked Daisy, delighted by the idea.

'No, that place is where shepherds can stay. Lookers. That's what we call 'em on the Marsh. So when they 'ave to stay out overnight, they can 'ave themselves a fire and a place to stretch their legs, out of the rain.'

'But I don't see any sheep,' said Peter.

Adam snorted. 'There's still some around, but they go where they've a mind to,' he said. 'There's no fences nor nothin' to keep 'em in. So you'll see huts like that all over the Marsh. Quite a few of 'em are still in use. They goes back to the Middle Ages, they does, round the time of the Great Plague.'

'What's the Great Plague?' asked Daisy nervously.

'Oh, it's just something that happened hundreds of years ago,' Peter told her, not wanting to give her too much information. He knew how she worried about such things. 'But don't fret, things from the past can't harm you.'

'Amen to that,' said Mrs Beesley and Peter noticed that she surreptitiously made the sign of the cross. He wondered why she was so scared and what she was trying to ward off.

The cart rumbled on, for what must have been miles. The sun finally began to sink below the horizon and, as the light diminished, the temperature dropped abruptly. Peter was obliged to drape the smelly travel blanket around Daisy and himself again. As darkness gathered, a low mist rose up from the wide expanses of grass on either side of them, thick tendrils of grey curling in over the edges of the track, until the cart appeared to be moving across a rippling ocean of fog.

'The light's almost gone,' observed Mrs Beesley and Peter could detect something new in her voice. Where she had previously sounded anxious, now she seemed terrified.

'We'll be all right,' Adam assured her. 'It's only a couple of miles.'

'We need to go quicker,' insisted Mrs Beesley. She leaned suddenly across him and snatched up the whip in her hand. 'If you won't use this thing, I shall!' she snarled.

'Give it 'ere,' growled Adam crossly. 'You'll have some-body's eye out with it.' He took the whip from her and then cracked it expertly above Bessie's head, causing her to lunge forward a little faster than before.

'Don't hurt the horse!' protested Daisy.

'I shan't,' Adam promised her. 'I wouldn't 'urt old Bessie. Me and 'er have been together too long.'

'What's the big worry about being out in the dark?' asked Peter.

There was a long uncomfortable silence and then Mrs Beesley said, 'We could go off the road in this mist and break an axle. Then we'd be stuck, wouldn't we? We'd 'ave to walk.' The explanation should have been convincing enough, but something in her voice seemed evasive. What's more, her anxiety was infectious. Now Peter turned to look at the west to see that the last of the sun was just disappearing over the horizon. Darkness spilled like a great shadow over the world. It wrapped itself around them like a chill cloak, and Peter was aware of his own breath clouding as it left his mouth.

And then he heard it. It was distant but clear as a bell. It was the sound of music playing, a single instrument, a flute perhaps, or a recorder, playing a slow, sweet melody. It rose and fell on the night air and there was something about the tune that was strangely familiar, oddly compelling. It seemed to be calling to him, somehow, inviting him to go and find the source of the music.

'What's that?' asked Peter nervously.

'What's what?' asked Mrs Beesley, keeping her gaze fixed resolutely on the way ahead.

'That...music,' said Daisy.

Mrs Beesley glanced at them briefly, then looked away. 'Can't 'ear none,' she assured them.

'But...you must. It's really clear.' Peter glared at Mrs Beesley but she kept her eyes fixed in front of her. 'Adam? You can hear it, can't you?'

'Oh, that...that's just the wind stirrin' the branches of the trees.'

Peter gazed around at the barren mist-covered wilderness all around him. 'But there aren't any trees,' he said.

Adam didn't answer. Instead, he lifted the whip and cracked it over Bessie's head a second time, but it didn't seem to have much effect. Then Mrs Beesley said something under her breath. She snatched the whip from his hand and brought it down lower so the leather flail snapped against Bessie's back, causing her to lunge forward with renewed speed.

'Don't,' cried Daisy. 'You said you wouldn't hurt her!'

But Mrs Beesley ignored her. She raised the whip again and brought it down with a crack like a rifle shot and now Bessie was almost galloping, the shuddering cart threatening to break itself to pieces on the uneven road. The darkness deepened. The music seemed to grow louder still, as though the two things were somehow linked, the lilting refrain repeating itself over and over, rising above the clattering of the wheels and the pounding of Bessie's hooves.

'What *is* that?' cried Peter; but the two adults were hunched forward in their seats, their gazes intent on the way ahead.

'There!' cried Adam, pointing. Rising up from the misty stretch ahead of them was a dark shape. At first it was indistinct, but as they raced nearer, Peter could see that it was the front of a two-storey house with what looked like a thatched roof. Closer still and Peter could discern a dull light in a couple of the ground-floor windows and a slow plume of grey smoke spilling from one of the chimneys. Finally, he was able to pick out the shape of a pair of stone gateposts, some distance in front of the house, at the top of a long drive. The cart rattled through the entrance and went along the drive, gravel crunching beneath the wheels. They passed through beautifully tended lawns and entered a flagged courtyard. Adam pulled back on the reins, telling Bessie to stop, which she did with evident relief. Her flanks were shiny with sweat and Peter noticed with a hint of disgust that a couple of spots were streaked with red where the whip had caught her.

'You hurt her!' cried Daisy again. 'You said you wouldn't.'

Adam turned to look at her, his face expressionless, as though he was in some kind of trance. Peter saw that despite the chill of the evening, the man's ruddy face was shiny with sweat. 'I'm sorry,' he muttered. 'We ... we couldn't risk being stuck out there.'

Mrs Beesley gave a dismissive snort and pushed the whip back into Adam's hands. Then she swung her heavy frame down from the seat. 'See to the pony,' she said. 'And get a grip on yourself.' She turned back to look at the passengers, that fake smile on her face again. 'Now, come along, children, let's get you inside where it's nice and warm.'

Peter and Daisy clambered down, but as he did so, Peter became aware of the music again, rising and falling from somewhere out on the Marsh. The shrill tones almost seemed to echo. He turned to look back that way, but the mist was so thick now, he couldn't see more than twenty yards in front of him.

'What a weird tune,' he muttered.

'I like it,' said Daisy dreamily.

But then Mrs Beesley took each of their arms and pulled them towards the front door of the house. Pushing it open, she led them inside.

CHAPTER FIVE

The children found themselves in a narrow hallway. On one wall, a large clock was ticking loudly. Through a half-open doorway to their right, Peter could see a large living room, with an inviting coal fire blazing in a cast-iron hearth; and slumped in a chair by the fire sat a grey-haired man, who seemed to be deep in thought as he stared into the dancing flames. A wireless was playing in there, some kind of syrupy dance music, but the man didn't really seem to be listening to it. Peter half expected to be ushered into the room and introduced to the man, but instead Mrs Beesley beckoned them onwards, along the hall to a tiled kitchen at the back of the house. A black cooking range filled the place with a muggy heat. She indicated a large pine table around which were placed six wooden chairs.

'Now, you two take your coats off and sit yourselves down,' she suggested. 'I'll find you summat to eat. And you'd like a cup of hot tea, I expect.' She walked over to a brown Philco battery-powered wireless standing on a small table and switched it on. After a few moments, the sounds of music filled the kitchen, the same programme that had been playing in the other room, Peter decided. 'I likes a bit of music, don't you?' said Mrs Beesley, with that forced jollity in her voice, but she didn't wait to hear a reply. She hung her coat on a peg on the back of the door and tied a white apron round her stout waist. Then she placed a big, black kettle onto the hotplate of the stove and strode over to a spacious pantry. She went inside and her disembodied voice floated out to them. 'It'll only be cold meat and bread, I'm afraid. It's a little late to start cookin'.'

Peter and Daisy settled themselves at the table. Daisy looked exhausted, Peter thought, and he didn't feel much better. He watched as Mrs Beesley emerged, carrying a couple of covered plates. She set them down on a worktop, took a sharp knife from a drawer and set to work, slicing thick pieces of ham from a large joint.

'Who was that man?' asked Peter.

Mrs Beesley didn't look up from her work. 'What man?' she asked.

'Sitting in the other room when we came in.'

'Oh, that's Mr Sheldon. We shan't bother him tonight, he's a little...preoccupied.'

'What's "proccypied"?' whispered Daisy, and Peter could only shrug his shoulders.

'I'll introduce you to him tomorrow mornin',' continued Mrs Beesley. 'At breakfast. He'll want to have a quick word with you, I expect. And you'll be introduced to Sally, of course.'

'Sally?' Peter looked at her blankly.

'Mr Sheldon's daughter. She'll be asleep now. She's not well, poor thing. She's better in the daytime.' She moved over to a large bread bin and took out a crusty loaf. She cut two thick slices and spread them liberally with bright yellow butter. 'Now then,' she said. 'That should keep the wolf from the door.'

Daisy looked at Peter, alarmed. 'There are *wolves*?' she gasped.

Peter smiled, shook his head. 'She just means it'll fill us up,' he explained. 'There *are* no wolves in England. Not any more.'

'Did there used to be?'

'Oh yes, in the olden times.'

'Like Red Riding Hood?'

'Umm . . . sort of.'

'And did they eat grandmothers?'

'No, that's just a story.'

Mrs Beesley brought over a couple of plates and set them down on the table. 'Eat hearty,' she suggested.

They needed no second bidding. They were ravenous. Peter slapped a large slice of ham onto the bread, folded it over and took a huge bite. Daisy followed suit, but ate in her own way, tearing small pieces and popping them daintily into her mouth. As he chewed, Peter gazed around the room, noticing that the only light in here came from a couple of paraffin lamps standing at each end of the room. They gave a dull, yellow glow, quite unlike the electric bulbs they used at home. Through a small, leaded window, he could just make out the pale branches of a tree stirring in the wind. It occurred to him that it was the first real tree he'd seen since they'd got off the train.

Steam began to spill from the kettle and Mrs Beesley filled a teapot. She brought it to the table on a tray with three cups, a large jug of milk and a bowl of sugar. She took one of the empty seats. 'We'll just let that steep for a bit,' she announced. 'I likes my tea strong. How about you two?'

'Daisy doesn't drink tea,' said Peter, talking with a mouth

full of bread and meat. 'She prefers milk. I like my tea strong with milk and two sugars, please.'

'Aren't you nice and polite?' said Mrs Beesley. 'It's a pleasure to hear somebody with proper manners.' She filled one of the mugs with milk and slid it across the table to Daisy. 'There you are, my dear. And me and Peter will wait a little bit for ours.' She studied Peter thoughtfully for a moment. 'Now, before we go much further, we should talk about the rules of the 'ouse.'

'Rules?' said Peter. He took another bite of his bread.

'Oh, don't worry, there aren't many of 'em,' Mrs Beesley assured him. 'The main thing is this. Out there...' She pointed to the window and the swaying branches of the tree. 'Out there is one of the biggest marshes on God's earth. I suppose you know what a marsh is?'

Daisy shook her head. 'Is it a kind of animal?' she asked.

'No, it's not,' Peter corrected her. 'A marsh is an area of boggy ground. I read that in the children's encyclopaedia. Dagenham used to be a marsh, in the olden days. Mr Griffiths told me that. The Thames used to flood from time to time.'

'Is that right?' said Mrs Beesley. 'Well then, Peter, you'll know that marshes can be treacherous. Out there, there's all kinds of things...lakes, canals, ponds...even quicksand.'

'Quicksand?' Daisy's eyes got big and round. 'We saw that in a film once, didn't we, Peter? A cowboy film. Are there cowboys here?'

Mrs Beesley laughed, shook her head. 'Bless you, my dear, that's one thing that's in very short supply. There's only shepherds in these parts and even they're gettin' pretty thin on the ground. But you mind my words now, a marsh can be a right dangerous place. You might think you can see where water is, but sometimes you can't. You have to stick to the paths, and if you don't know where those paths are, well... you could easily come a cropper.'

Peter frowned. 'Does that mean we can never go out?'

'I'm not sayin' that. Adam knows the paths better'n anyone and he'll most likely take you out in the daytime and show you the safe tracks.'

Peter pushed his empty plate aside. 'Is that why you were so frightened before? In case the cart ended up in quicksand?'

'Bless you, child, I wasn't *frightened*,' said Mrs Beesley, with an unconvincing laugh. 'But... yes, that's what I was worried about. There's more'n a few carts come to grief over the years. Terrible accidents.' She eyed the teapot. 'That tea should be about ready now,' she said. She lifted the teapot and filled the other two cups, then added a splash of milk and two teaspoons of sugar to Peter's. She slid it across the table and he raised it to his lips and sipped at it thankfully.

He remembered something that had temporarily slipped his mind and he pulled the postcard from the coat that was draped over the back of his chair. 'I need the address,' he said. 'So I can tell Mum where we are.'

'You just hold your 'orses,' said Mrs Beesley. She reached out and took the card from him. 'I'll fill in the address for you when I've a spare moment. And you can write a little message tellin' your mother 'ow you're gettin' on. But we won't be able to post it for a few days, not until we go into the market at Hythe.' She noticed Peter's outraged expression. 'You're not in Lunnen now,' she told him. 'Hythe is a town, it's where the nearest post office is.'

Peter wasn't happy at this news. 'Mum will be worried,' he said.

'Not at all. Great big boy like you! I should think your mother has enough to worry about, what with the war comin' and everything.' She sighed. 'It beats me why people can't just...get along,' she said. 'That Mr Hitler, what does he think he's playin' at?'

The question hung for a moment but Peter didn't think he had much of an answer for it. 'My dad was called up,' he said at last. 'He's gone off to learn to be a soldier.' An image flashed into his mind: his father's face when they'd seen him off at the station, pale and drawn, but trying to pretend that everything was fine. He'd smiled at Daisy, a most unconvincing smile, and Peter could tell that he was filled with dread inside. It was very much like the cheerful bluster that Mrs Beesley had attempted when she claimed she hadn't been frightened out on the Marsh.

Mrs Beesley shook her head. 'You'd have thought the last one would have put 'em off such notions,' she said. '"The War To End All Wars", they called it. Didn't work though, did it? Of course, I was just a young thing when all that started. My father and my brothers all marched off to fight the Hun. Not a single one of 'em come back.' She realised what she was saying and hastily added, 'Not that such a thing will happen to your father! They say it'll all be different this time. No mud, no trenches...a gentlemen's war, that's what they say t'will be.' She noticed that Daisy's eyelids were drooping. 'Here, listen to me going on and that little girl is nearly fallin' asleep where she sits! Finish up that tea, Peter, and the two of you gather your things. I'll show you where you'll be sleepin'.

CHAPTER SIX

Peter and Daisy followed Mrs Beesley up the creaking wooden staircase. She was carrying an oil lamp, the only source of light. Burdened with their cases and gas masks, it was hard for the children to see where they were going. When they had reached the first floor, Mrs Beesley indicated a closed door near the top of the stairs and lowered her voice to a theatrical whisper. 'That's Miss Sally's room,' she hissed. 'You're not to go disturbing her unless you check it's all right with me first.' She pointed along the landing to another door. 'That there's the throne room,' she said.

Daisy looked up at her, nonplussed. 'The what?' she asked.

'Oh, you know. The...little room, the smallest room in the house...'

'I think she means the lavatory,' said Peter.

'Yes, thank you, Peter.' Mrs Beesley looked disapproving, as though the very mention of such a word was too much for her. 'If you have to pay a visit during the night, be as quiet as you can. These old floorboards creak somethin' terrible.' She led them onwards. 'Daisy, you'll be in this room, right next door to Sally. Hold on a moment while I go in and light the other lamp.'

'Don't you have 'lectric here?' asked Daisy.

'No, my dear, not yet. It'd cost the electric company far too much to bring it way out here. But Mr Sheldon 'as said, just as soon as it becomes available, we'll have it installed.'

She went into the room, taking the only source of light with her and the two children had no option but to wait in almost total darkness. Daisy pressed a little closer to her brother. 'I don't like this,' she whispered.

'Don't worry, it's only for a minute or two. I expect...' He broke off at the distant sound of music, coming from somewhere outside, the same slow melody he had heard before. He hadn't been able to hear it downstairs with the wireless playing, but up here in the silence of the landing, it was different. 'What *is* that?' he muttered. 'It seems to be...'

He stopped at a sound coming from Miss Sally's room, the urgent clanking of metal against metal. He and Daisy looked at each other, puzzled.

'What's that?' whispered Daisy fearfully.

'I don't know,' admitted Peter. 'It sounds like—'

'You can come in now,' announced Mrs Beesley, interrupting him. Peter pushed Daisy ahead of him into the room. He heard her give a gasp of surprise, and a moment later he understood why. The room was large and lavishly decorated, lit now by the glow of two paraffin lamps. Mrs Beesley was standing beside a tall mahogany wardrobe. A huge four-poster bed stood in the middle of the room, hung with swathes of red velvet, and at the foot of it there was a magnificent dapple-grey rocking horse, its teeth bared, its eyes wild. But what really caught Peter's attention were the dolls.

There were scores of them, all sitting and staring blankly towards the door, as though they'd somehow been expecting Daisy, their little mouths curved into grins revealing shiny white porcelain teeth. There were dolls of every size. They were sitting on shelves, on benches, on window seats, even on the floor along the base of the wall. A couple of larger ones sat on the bed propped up against the pillows. There were pretty female dolls with big blue eyes, blonde tresses and silk gowns. There were clown dolls with painted faces and garish outfits. There were African dolls and Spanish dolls and Japanese dolls and just about any other nationality you could think of. Against one wall stood a huge, ornate dolls' house, four storeys high, and on each floor little pale faces peered from every window and every doorway, as though judging the new arrivals.

Daisy stood for a moment looking around in silent amazement, her eyes big and wide as she took in every detail. Then she ran into the room, entranced.

'Oh, Peter, look at them! Aren't they *lovely*?'

Peter frowned. He knew that his sister loved dolls, that she was always asking her mother if she might have another to be a companion for Eva. So this room must have been her idea of heaven. But this...this was simply too much. Peter could somehow feel the power of all of those glass eyes staring at him and he felt decidedly uncomfortable under their gaze. Daisy made a beeline for the dolls' house and unlatched a door, lifting a hand to reach in and take one out.

'No!' snapped Mrs Beesley, and Daisy froze as if she'd been slapped. 'Ah no, we don't play with the dolls, Daisy. We can *look* at them, but we don't ever touch them.'

Daisy looked crestfallen. 'Oh but...they're *dolls*. Can't I...?'

Mrs Beesley shook her head. She moved closer and

reached out an arm to push the dolls' house door firmly shut. 'They are very valuable,' she explained. 'They have to be kept just as they are. Miss Sally is most particular about it.'

There was a puzzled silence. Peter could imagine Daisy asking herself the inevitable question. *What's the point of having dolls you can't play with?*

He asked one himself. 'Who do they belong to?'

'Why, these are very old,' said Mrs Beesley. 'Been in this house since the 1800s, they have. Aren't they pretty? Miss Sally loves these dolls. Used to spend all her time in 'ere, she did. Not playin' with 'em, you understand. Just lookin' at 'em. Talkin' to 'em. That kind of thing.' She smiled, remembering something. 'D'you know, she used to tell me that one of the dolls used to speak to her, just as clear as I'm speaking now? Sally says she used to talk right back to it.' She turned to study the dolls for a moment as though trying to spot the likely culprit but she shook her head. 'There's so many of 'em, it's impossible to remember which one,' she said. 'Tillie, I believe Miss Sally called her.' She looked back at Daisy, as though dismissing Peter. 'Now, dear, you can unpack all your things and put them in the wardrobe there. Then get yourself ready for—'

'The dolls must have belonged to *somebody*,' insisted Peter. He wasn't prepared to let Mrs Beesley talk her way around this one.

Mrs Beesley looked back at him, an expression of irritation on her face. 'Well, if you must know, they belonged to one of Miss Sally's ancestors,' she said. 'A girl called Alison. Miss Sally inherited them when she was born.' A troubled look came to her ruddy face. 'You know, at one time, Mr Sheldon was all for getting rid of the dolls. Said he was sick of them cluttering up the place. And some antiques fellow he met had looked at them and made quite a handsome offer for them. But Miss Sally wouldn't hear of it. Begged and pleaded she did, worked herself up into a right old state until he finally gave in to her. He always does in the end. They are very valuable. So I must ask you, Daisy, not to touch them, there's a good girl.'

Daisy nodded glumly. She had sat down on the bed and opened her own suitcase. She took out Eva and sat her on the bed, propped up against the pillows.

'And who have we here?' asked Mrs Beesley.

'This is Eva. She's my doll,' said Daisy quietly. And then she added fearfully. 'I *can* play with her, can't I?'

'Why, of course you can, silly! You don't imagine I'd stop

you from playing with your own doll, do you? I'm not a monster, you know. Do I seem like a monster to you?'

There was an uncomfortable silence.

'Yes, well...' Mrs Beesley looked around the room, as if to assure herself that everything was in perfect order. Then she looked at Peter and, picking up one of the lamps, she added, in a businesslike tone, 'Now, if you'd like to come with me, young man, I'll show you where you'll be spending the night.'

CHAPTER SEVEN

Peter's room was nothing like Daisy's. Tucked away under the eaves of the roof on the second floor, it was a small, spartan affair with a single bed and a cheap pine wardrobe. A jug of water and a washbasin stood on a mahogany stand. Peter told himself that at least he didn't have a whole army of dolls staring at him while he slept. There were no other lights up here, apart from the paraffin lamp that Mrs Beesley had used to light their way up the stairs, but she produced a box of Vestas from the pocket of her apron and set light to a candle in a tin holder on the bedside table, placing the box of matches down beside it.

'Blow the candle out before you go to sleep,' she warned him. 'We don't want any fires, do we? I'll leave the matches here in case you need to go to the...' (She couldn't seem to bring herself to say the word 'lavatory') '...the little room. Now, are you all set?' she asked him.

Peter nodded and stood there rather forlornly, not sure what to do. At home he always had a hug from Mum before he turned in, but there was no way he was going to attempt that with Mrs Beesley, even if she'd wanted one.

'Well, I'll be off then,' she said. 'I'll give you a call in the morning.' She threw him a stern look. 'It won't be none of them Lunnen hours, mind,' she said. 'We're early risers in this house.' She picked up her lamp and went out, closing the door behind her. After a few moments, he heard the sound of her feet clumping down the stairs.

Peter was alone in the tiny, low-roofed room. There was no window to look out from, just a small skylight with a view of a handful of scattered stars. He got his pyjamas from his case and changed quickly into them, then brushed his teeth and there being no sink, spat the water into the washbasin. It was cold in the room, so he pulled back the sheets and climbed into the unfamiliar bed. He stared at the ceiling above his head, which bore a large stain, the shape of which made him think of a map of India he'd seen back in school.

The day's events flashed through his mind in a mad jumble of images and sounds, but he was so exhausted he soon found that the memories were dissolving into each other, becoming all mixed up. Then he was drifting down into sleep but just before he was quite gone, his senses picked up a faint sound, somewhere in the house. Once again, it sounded like metal clanking against metal, as though somebody was repeatedly rattling a length of chain and he was pretty sure it was coming from Miss Sally's room. He had time enough to think how odd it was to hear such a thing indoors before sleep stole over him like a warm, enveloping blanket. But hidden in its folds was one of the most unsettling dreams he had ever experienced.

He was out on the Marsh in the bright sunshine, strolling across a wide flat meadow. He felt deliciously wicked being out here on his own, because he'd been told it was forbidden, but there had been something so inviting about walking out in the heat of this Indian summer that it was too compelling to resist. Nevertheless, he kept telling himself to be careful, because Adam had warned him you couldn't always see where the water was...

But then he *did* see water, a wide straight line of it cutting across the land in front of him, its banks too regular to be a natural river. A canal, he supposed; Adam had said something about canals, had even warned him not to go near them, but this one seemed harmless enough. He approached the bank and stared into the still, olive-green water. The water was flanked by rows of trees, rich in summer foliage, and Peter found himself thinking that it was nice to see them, he'd seen so few since his arrival on the Marsh. Birds fluttered in amongst the branches, their wings blurring and the air was filled with their melodic songs.

He sighed and began to stroll along the bank, his hands in his pockets. He was enjoying the feel of the sun on his face and he saw no reason why he shouldn't stroll this way for miles, enjoying the calm and the solitude. And then he noticed something prowling towards him along the bank of the canal: a sleek, dark shape. He realised with a flash of apprehension that it was a wolf. At the moment, it didn't seem to be aware of him, but soon, he was sure, it would lift its head and those cold eyes would alight on him.

Peter looked helplessly around. He considered running back in the direction from which he had come, but he didn't doubt for a moment that the wolf, with its long, slender legs, would run him down in seconds. Then he noticed a boat beached on the bank of the canal, a simple wooden skiff with a battered-looking oar lying in the bottom of it. He stood there, gazing down at the boat, remembering that

Adam had warned him to stay away from the water, but at the same time reminding himself that a wolf was coming, a ravenous beast that might tear him limb from limb, if given a chance.

Suddenly, inexplicably, he was *in* the boat and it was moving slowly downriver, pushed along by the slightest of breezes. Peter looked up and saw that he was moving on past the wolf and that the creature was standing on the bank of the canal gazing at him, calmly and placidly, and he realised then that the wolf had never meant him any harm. Indeed, the expression in its grey eyes was one of compassion, as though the creature somehow felt sorry for him.

In a few moments the boat had moved on, leaving the wolf behind. Peter decided that now he was here, he might as well enjoy the experience. So he reached out a hand and trailed it in the water, expecting to feel the cold shock of it against his fingers, but it was as warm and comforting as a Sunday night bath. He sighed and laid himself down in the bottom of the boat, gazing up at the shimmering blue sky above him, the flocks of birds wheeling and soaring on the warm air. He felt sleepy and thought that he might have a nap.

And then he felt something bump against the underside of the boat. He sat up in surprise and looked over the side to see that the skiff had become entangled in a straggle of thick green weed, growing just below the surface. He reached out and took hold of a handful of the swaying fronds, tugged at them in an attempt to free the boat. They were thick and fleshy and had a disagreeably slimy feel to them. Peter frowned, renewed his efforts. If he didn't free the boat, he'd be stuck here and, somehow, he didn't fancy the idea of swimming through that dark water. He renewed his efforts but couldn't seem to get a proper grip. And then he noticed something else, something that was tangled in the weeds, long strands of a fine straw-coloured substance that was rippling and swaying in the water. Curious, he leaned closer and, grabbing a handful of it, he gave it a firm tug. He felt something bump again against the underside of the boat, so he pulled harder, and this time, whatever it was, rolled around the curve of the boat and came bobbing to the surface.

He saw too much, too quickly – a bleached white face, the eyes tight shut – and something moving in the open gaping mouth. Some kind of an eel, Peter thought, but he didn't want to think about that because now the thing in the water lifted a shrivelled arm and pointed a finger at him. Lost in panic, his heart hammering in his chest, Peter registered that the eyes of the face in the water were now open and that they were twinkling with what looked like amusement. Then from the creature's open mouth came the gurgling, bubbling sound of mocking laughter...

CHAPTER EIGHT

Grandad Peter stops talking suddenly. Helen is sitting forward in the rocking chair, one hand clamped over her mouth, from which has just issued a gasp of pure terror.

'Are you all right?' he asks her.

She stares back at him. 'Weren't you terrified?'

He shrugs. 'Not at first,' he assures her. 'It seemed real as it was happening, but dreams are always like that, aren't they? So convincing. So ... believable. But then, when you wake up and everything seems normal again ... the feeling fades. It's only later, much later, when other things fall into place, that you realise the dream actually meant something. That it was more than it seemed. A warning, I suppose. And I'll never know who or what was trying to give me that warning but ... I'm convinced now that's exactly what it was.'

His voice trails away and he studies Helen for a moment.

THE PIPER

'Perhaps you don't really want to hear any more,' he suggests. 'Maybe I should leave it there.'

She shakes her head. 'No, please. Go on. What happened next?'

Grandad Peter thinks for a moment, as though trying to remember. Then his eyes widen slightly, as the details return to him.

He continues with his story.

CHAPTER NINE

Peter woke with a gasp and, for a few moments, he didn't know where he was. He lay there, his heart thumping like a steam hammer in his chest while he told himself repeatedly, *It was just a dream. It was just a dream . . .*

Then bit by bit, it all came back to him . . . the station early that morning, the train journey, the Friends' Meeting House, that nightmarish ride across the Marsh to Sheldon Grange . . .

He looked quickly around the little room. Sunlight was streaming in through the skylight and he could hear birds singing out there in the world.

He realised that somebody had just knocked on the door of his room.

'H . . . hello?' he murmured.

'Time to get up, Peter,' announced Mrs Beesley's strident voice. 'The day's almost over. And give that sister of yours a shout while you're at it. I knocked on 'er door but I didn't get an answer.'

'Er... right, Mrs Beesley. I'm on my way.' He flung aside the covers, got out of bed and dressed himself hurriedly, realising that his hopes for a leisurely holiday in the country were clearly not to be. He went down to the next floor and after a visit to the lavatory, he walked along the landing to Daisy's room. He tapped on the door but there was no sound from within, so he turned the handle and went inside.

Daisy was lying on her back in the huge bed, her blonde hair fanned on the pillow. As he drew closer, he could see that she was still asleep, her eyes closed. She had a doll cradled in her arms, hugged in close to her face and Peter was surprised to see that it wasn't Eva, but one of the 'valuable' dolls from the window seat, a tiny figure with black hair and a white, china head. The bright-green glass eyes of the doll looked somehow too big for her face. Peter frowned, wondering what Mrs Beesley would have to say about it if she knew. He reached out to try and prise the doll carefully out of Daisy's grip, but as he did so, Daisy spoke, making him start.

'No, it's not,' she said, sounding rather cross. 'Well, you would say that, wouldn't you?'

Peter smiled. She was talking in her sleep, but quite clearly, as though in the middle of a conversation.

'Daisy?' he murmured.

A pause. 'But I'm not *supposed* to go out at night. It's not safe.' Another lengthy pause, as though she was listening to a reply. Then: 'I don't know. I'll have to think about it. I'll see what Peter says.'

'Daisy!' Peter reached out a hand and shook his sister's shoulder. She awoke suddenly, looking startled.

'What's the matter?' she asked crossly, glaring at him.

'Time to get up, sleepyhead. You were talking in your sleep.'

'Was not.'

'Were too!'

Now Daisy was looking in surprise at the doll in her hands. 'Why did you put this here?' she asked. 'Mrs Beesley said I wasn't to touch the dolls. She'll be angry if she finds out.'

'I didn't do anything,' he assured her. 'I just came in the room this minute. Here.' He reached out, took the doll from her and walked over to the window seat, where he slotted it into an empty space amongst the others. He looked out of the window. It was a bright, sunny morning but the grounds of the Grange appeared to be deserted. He turned back to look at Daisy.

She struggled into a sitting position and stared slowly around the room, blinking like an owl. She looked dazed, still half asleep.

'Where's Eva?' she asked him.

'I don't know,' he said. He looked around the room and then saw Daisy's regular doll lying face down on the wooden floor beside the bed, half hidden by a fold of bedcovers. 'Here she is,' he announced, and he stooped to pick her up. 'Oh,' he said, dismayed.

Eva's black face had a big jagged crack across the middle.

Daisy glared at him. 'What have you done?' she shrieked.

'I haven't done anything,' he protested. 'She must have fallen off the bed in the night.' He stepped forward and handed her the damaged doll. 'What a shame,' he said.

Daisy cradled the doll in her arms and her eyes filled with tears. 'Poor Eva,' she wailed. 'I promised I'd look after you and now see what's happened.'

'I expect Mum and Dad will buy you a new doll as soon as we get home,' Peter assured her.

'I don't *want* a new doll. I want Eva.'

Peter sighed. This morning wasn't going very well so far.

He studied his sister for a moment. 'Daisy, were you dreaming just now?'

She shook her head sullenly. 'Why?' she muttered.

'It's just that when I came in you were...well, it was as though you were talking to somebody.'

She didn't say anything, so he added, 'You'd better get up and dressed.' He smiled, made an attempt to be jovial. 'You're not in Lunnen now!'

'It's *London*,' she corrected him, her face arranged into a scowl.

'What's wrong with you this morning?'

'I didn't get much sleep.'

'You were doing a pretty good job of it when I came in,' he assured her. 'And talking to somebody.'

'Was NOT!'

He sighed. He wasn't going to get into that again. 'Well, anyway, you'd better move yourself, before the old battle-axe comes looking for you. I'll see you downstairs.' He walked to the door and then turned back to look at her. She was still cradling Eva. Beyond her, the other dolls watched her in silence. There was something about the intensity of their concerted gaze that unsettled Peter. 'Don't be all day,' he said and he went out of the room, closing the door behind him.

Just as he was about to walk away, he quite distinctly heard Daisy say, 'Why did you do that? That wasn't very nice!'

A shiver of apprehension went through him. He hesitated, on the point of opening the door again and going back inside, but something stopped him. Because he knew that if he went back in there, Daisy would look at him with those big, innocent eyes and ask him what he was talking about. He felt a strange sense of foreboding within him and he thought about the dream he'd had, that hideous pale face rising up out of the water...

He shook his head to dispel the last traces of sleep and went downstairs to face a new day.

CHAPTER TEN

He found Mrs Beesley in the kitchen, standing at the cooking range over a sizzling frying pan. The room was rich with the appetising aroma of bacon and he felt his stomach gurgle in anticipation. She looked up from her work for a moment and nodded him towards the kitchen table. 'Take a seat,' she said. 'Where's that sister of yours?'

'She'll be down in a moment,' he said. 'I don't think she slept too well.'

Mrs Beesley grunted. 'First night in a new house, that's not unusual,' she said. She cracked open an egg with an expert one-handed flourish and dropped it into the frying pan. 'An old place like this, there's all kinds of noises at night. Creaks, rattles...and then there's outside. Owls hooting, winds a-blowing...noises you might never identify.' She cracked a second egg and dropped it in beside the other one. She took a spoon and drizzled hot fat over the yolks, then lifted her head as Daisy trudged into the kitchen, rubbing her eyes. 'Ah, now here's madam,' she observed. 'I 'ope you're feeling hungry. Got a good old country breakfast for you.'

Daisy took a seat next to Peter. 'Eva got broken,' she said moodily.

'Eva?'

'Her doll,' explained Peter. 'I think it fell off the bed.'

'Oh, that's a shame. Perhaps I'll get Adam to look at it for you. He's very handy with a tube of glue, that man.'

'Where *is* Adam?' asked Peter.

'He has his breakfast out in the stable,' she told him. 'Sleeps out there as well. We don't allow him in the house too often.'

Peter frowned. 'Why not?' he asked.

'He's just a hired hand,' said Mrs Beesley, as though that explained everything, but Peter didn't really understand what she meant. Surely, if *she* wasn't part of the Sheldon family, then she was a hired hand too?

She served up two plates of sausage, egg and bacon and brought them over to the table, setting them down in front of the children.

'That'll stick to yer ribs,' she assured them.

'Thank you,' said Peter. He picked up his knife and fork and set to with gusto, but he knew that Daisy was more finicky than him. She sat there, staring at her plate but making no attempt to eat.

'What's the matter with you?' asked Mrs Beesley. 'It's eggs and bacon. You have that in Lunnen, don't you?'

'Mummy always breaks my yolk for me,' said Daisy quietly, and Peter nudged her under the table with one foot. He reached over and sliced open her egg with his knife, causing the yolk to ooze across the plate.

'There,' he said. 'All done.'

Daisy continued to gaze at her plate. 'But now it's all runny,' she complained. She looked at Mrs Beesley. 'Do you have any ketchup?' she asked.

'I should think not!' said Mrs Beesley, as though she'd asked for something illegal. 'I don't 'old with that new-fangled stuff. That's how we eat 'em on the Marsh, take it or leave it.'

Daisy sighed and picking up her cutlery, she began to pick half-heartedly at the food.

Mrs Beesley returned to the range and busied herself for a few moments. She came back with a cup of tea for Peter and a glass of milk for Daisy. She watched as Peter spooned sugar into his cup.

'Enjoy it while you can,' she advised him. 'Everyone's saying that stuff'll be rationed before very much longer.'

'What's *rationed*?' asked Daisy.

'It's when they only let you have so much of something,' said Peter. 'Like one lump of sugar a day or one slice of bacon a week.'

'I shouldn't like that,' said Daisy, lifting a dainty scrap of bacon to her mouth. Peter placed a whole rasher onto a slice of bread and butter, folded it across the middle and began to eat it in large hungry bites.

'You eat like a wolf,' complained Daisy and he was reminded of his dream.

'Nothing wrong with a healthy appetite,' said Mrs Beesley. 'That boy's going to need his energy if he's to make himself useful around the place. Peter was telling me you didn't sleep too well,' she added, reaching for another cup.

'Not really,' said Daisy. 'The girls woke me up.'

Mrs Beesley didn't turn, but Peter noticed how her body tensed at this. 'Girls?' she muttered.

'Yes, the ones who were dancing in the garden last night.'

Peter saw the china cup slip from Mrs Beesley's fingers and fall to the tiled floor. It seemed to fall for a long time, long enough for him to anticipate the sound of it breaking to pieces and yet it still made him jump. Mrs Beesley looked down at the scattered pieces at her feet, as though she was completely surprised to see them there.

'Now look what I've gone and done,' she reproached herself. 'Bone china, that was.' She turned and glared at Daisy. 'Fancy saying such a silly thing,' she snapped. 'Girls, indeed!'

'But there *were* girls,' insisted Daisy. 'They were dancing to the music out in the garden. I saw them.'

'You couldn't have,' Peter told her. 'You must have been dreaming.'

'I wasn't even asleep,' she insisted. 'I heard that funny music playing again, so I got out of bed and I looked out of the window and there were two girls dancing on the lawn.'

'But that's silly,' insisted Peter. 'It was really late when we went to bed. You must have imagined it.'

Daisy responded as she usually did when challenged in this way. She started to cry. 'But I s-s-saw them,' she wailed.

Peter reacted instinctively. He put a hand on Daisy's shoulder and leaned closer to her. 'You know how you get bad dreams sometimes? And afterwards, you can't always tell what's a dream and what isn't.'

Saying this made an image flash through his mind – a bleached white face bobbing up to the surface of the canal. He had to close his eyes for a moment to try to rid himself of it.

'What's up with her?' demanded a gruff voice and Peter opened his eyes to see that a man had just strode into the room, the grey-haired man that Peter had glimpsed in the sitting room yesterday evening. He was short and stocky, dressed in a tweed jacket and trousers. Up close, Mr Sheldon looked ill, Peter thought, his face thin and haggard, his eyes rimmed with dark, fleshy pouches. He took a seat at the head of the table and sat there, gazing crossly at Daisy, as though the sound of her crying was annoying him. 'We don't want crying in this 'ouse,' he told Daisy. 'The wind might change and you'll be stuck like that.'

Daisy's mouth dropped open and she sat there regarding the man mournfully, gasping for breath as she tried to stop herself from weeping.

'She had a nightmare,' said Peter and was aware of Daisy looking at him, an expression of betrayal on her face.

'Is that all?' The man attempted a reassuring smile, but just like Mrs Beesley's earlier efforts, it was no more than a tightening of the muscles around the mouth. His eyes remained blank and expressionless. 'You'll be all right, my dear. I expect you're just homesick. Once you get used to the way we do things, you'll be right as rain, won't she, Mrs B?' He turned to look at his housekeeper to see that she was on her hands and knees, sweeping up the bits of broken crockery with a dustpan and brush. 'What happened there?' he asked.

'I dropped a cup,' she replied, not looking up at him. 'It was from the best set. I'm sorry, sir.'

He shrugged his shoulders. 'Not the end of the world,' he observed. 'There's worse things than a bit of broken crockery, a lot worse.'

'Yes, sir.'

He turned back to look at the children. 'I'm Mr Sheldon,' he told them. 'I own the Grange.'

'We're very pleased to meet you, sir,' said Peter, minding his manners, as he'd always been taught. 'This is my sister, Daisy.'

Daisy nodded silently.

'I thought I'd eat my breakfast with you this morning,' said Mr Sheldon. 'So we can have ourselves a little chat.' He tried the unconvincing smile again, then looked expectantly at Mrs Beesley. 'Mrs B?'

'Oh, of course, Mr Sheldon, I wasn't thinking.' In a flash, she was on her feet and back at the range, where she took a round metal cover off a plate and brought it to the table, holding it with an oven glove. It was a full English breakfast with sausages, bacon and two fried eggs. Mr Sheldon glanced at his plate, as though he couldn't be less interested and then, picking up his cutlery, he proceeded to push the food around, without actually putting any of it into his mouth. Peter noticed that his hands shook rather badly. After a few moments, Mr Sheldon lifted his gaze to Peter. 'So, how old are you, boy?' he asked.

'I'm thirteen, sir. I'll be fourteen in the spring.'

Mr Sheldon nodded. 'You look as though you're strong enough,' he said. 'You'll work with Adam, out on the Marsh.' It was not so much an invitation as a statement of fact. 'He'll show you how to guard the sheep and so forth. Show you where all the safe paths are. I expect you'll want to work to earn your keep?'

Peter nodded. 'Yes, sir. Thank you, sir,' he said, though he had to admit to himself that when he'd first heard about the evacuation, he'd anticipated having a bit of a holiday in the country, not a full-time job. 'What about school?' he asked.

Mr Sheldon looked at him. 'What about it?'

'We...will be going to school here...won't we?'

Mr Sheldon frowned. 'I'll look into it,' he said. 'The nearest schools are in Hythe and that's quite a trip. I would have thought you'd be glad to have a bit of time off. There's lots you can learn on a farm, y'know. Stuff you won't read in any book.' He turned his gaze to Daisy, who was finally calming down a little. 'As for you, young lady, you'll be a friend and companion for my daughter, Sally.' He thought for a moment, then glanced at Mrs Beesley. 'Have you told them anything about Sally?' he asked her.

'Only a little, Mr Sheldon. Just that she's not well.'

Mr Sheldon nodded and pushed his untouched food aside. 'Sally is...feverish,' he said. 'I think that's the best word to describe it. She's never been very strong and lately she's become prey to some strange notions. She...hears things. Has bad dreams. Fever dreams, I believe they're called. These days, she rarely leaves her room. What she needs is somebody to play with her...to spend time with her. She likes to be read to.' He looked concerned for a moment. 'I take it you *can* read?' he asked Daisy. She nodded sniffily. 'You're what, six years old?'

'Seven,' said Daisy. 'I'm the best reader in my class.'

'Good,' said Mr Sheldon. 'Excellent. Sally is eight,' he

added. 'Just a little bit older than you. I want you to be nice to her because she's all I've got in the world. Do you think you could do that for me?'

Daisy considered the question for a moment and then nodded her head, her expression grave. She was eating a little more steadily now as Mr Sheldon continued talking.

'You see, I worry about Sally. After what happened to her mother, I . . . well, I just can't . . . I *won't* allow anything bad to happen to her. She needs calm and quiet, especially at night . . . she needs to be able to sleep soundly and not be worrying about . . . about things she doesn't understand. She needs . . .' His voice trailed away and he sat there, staring at the table, as though trying to puzzle something out. Then he made an effort to pull himself together. 'Anyway,' he said, a strange, forced calm in his voice. 'Look at me sitting 'ere, chattering on with meself. I need to be gone. Work to do. There's always work. No rest for the wicked, eh?'

He got up from the table and Peter found himself thinking that judging by the age of his daughter, Mr Sheldon probably wasn't much older than his own father, but he looked elderly, a stooped frail old man weighed down by worry. 'I expect I'll see you both later,' he said tonelessly and shuffled out of the room.

Peter sat there, wondering what could have happened to Mr Sheldon to make him the way he was. And he wondered exactly what was wrong with his daughter. From what he'd just said, it was hard to be sure.

Mrs Beesley gathered up the empty plates and took them across to the sink. Mr Sheldon's untouched breakfast went straight into a swill bucket. Peter reflected what a terrible waste of food it was, but he was pretty full anyway and even Daisy had only managed to eat about half of her meal.

'Now,' said Mrs Beesley, turning away from the range. 'If you two have finished, we'll go on up and say hello to Miss Sally.'

CHAPTER ELEVEN

Peter and Daisy followed Mrs Beesley obediently back up the staircase. Daisy seemed to have forgotten all about the dream she'd had of the children in the garden. Perhaps the excitement of meeting somebody new had banished it from her mind, but Peter couldn't help wondering about it. It wasn't like Daisy to act this way. She'd always been so down to earth. And it wasn't really like him to have bad dreams. It must be something about this place, he decided.

They arrived at the top of the stairs and Mrs Beesley turned back to give them a meaningful look. 'Don't forget,' she whispered, 'Miss Sally is very delicate, so don't you be bothering her with too many of your daft notions.' Peter and Daisy exchanged baffled looks. They had no idea what this might mean, so they could only nod their heads in agreement.

Mrs Beesley reached out a hand and rapped her knuckles gently against the door. Then she opened it a few inches and peeked into the room. 'Miss Sally?' she said. 'I've brought our two guests to meet you. Are you well enough to receive visitors?'

'Yes,' said a faint voice from within. So Mrs Beesley opened the door fully and gestured for the two children to follow her into the room. It was as big as the one in which Daisy was staying, but happily completely devoid of dolls. Miss Sally, it seemed, was rather fond of reading, since three walls of the room were lined with bookshelves, all crammed with leather-bound volumes. Strangely, the main window of the room was boarded up with tightly nailed wooden panels, something which struck Peter as very odd, because it meant that a paraffin lamp had to be lit the whole time to provide illumination and because of this, the room had a stale, muggy atmosphere. Like Daisy's room, there was a huge four-poster bed in the centre of it and, lying in the bed, propped up on what looked like twenty lace-edged pillows, was Miss Sally herself. Peter had to admit that she did look rather ill. She was a plump girl with a pasty white complexion, dotted here and there with nasty-looking spots. She studied Peter and Daisy with her pale, rather watery hazel eyes. Her hair, a mass of red curls, lay fanned out on the pillows around her. She was clutching a book in her chubby hands and Peter could see the title, *Heidi Grows Up,* on the cover. She slipped a bookmark into the volume and set it down beside her on the bed, before directing a weak smile in the direction of her visitors. 'Hello,' she said.

'Now, Miss Sally,' said Mrs Beesley, 'allow me to introduce our guests from Lunnen. This is Daisy,' she said, pushing her a step closer, 'and this here is her brother, Peter. They're going to be spending some time with us. I'm sure you and Daisy will be *great* friends.' Peter noticed that there was no mention of him at this point, and was unsure if this meant that Mrs Beesley thought boys and girls couldn't actually *be* friends, but he made no comment. That was fine by him. 'I'll leave you all to get acquainted for a while,' continued Mrs Beesley. 'Peter, I'll be back for you in a bit. We'll see if Adam has a few odd jobs lined up for you.' She went out of the room, leaving the door slightly ajar.

There was an uncomfortable silence while the three of them regarded each other, trying to think of something to say, a situation that was soon resolved by Daisy, who stepped closer to the bed and pointed at the book. 'I loved *Heidi,*' she said. 'I read it at school. But I've never heard of *Heidi Grows Up.*'

'It's quite new,' said Sally. She gestured to an empty chair beside her bed and Daisy sat herself down on it. 'Of course, it's not even written by Johanna Spyri, it's by her translator, Charles Tritten. And you can tell it's not written by her because the style's not quite the same. But it's not bad. I have to have a book to read, otherwise life's not worth living.' She gestured around her. 'I've read every book in this room,' she announced with evident pride.

Peter gazed around in amazement. 'All of them?' he cried. 'That's amazing.'

Sally shrugged. 'I have to have something to keep me occupied,' she said. She smiled at Daisy and tapped the cover of the book beside her. 'I've only just started this one. Daddy got it for me when he went to Hythe. If you want, we can go back to the beginning and you can read it to me.'

Daisy nodded eagerly. 'I'd like that,' she said. 'Me and Peter saw the film of *Heidi*, didn't we, Peter? With Shirley Temple. It was on at the Regency. It wasn't as good as the book, but it wasn't *terrible*. Have you seen the film?'

Sally shook her head mournfully. 'I would have loved to,' she said. 'There's a cinema in Rye, but it didn't play there. And even if it came now, I'd be too ill to go. These days I don't get out at all. Daddy says it's for the best.'

'That must be *awful*,' said Daisy. She studied Sally

thoughtfully for a moment and then with typical bluntness asked, 'What's wrong with you?'

Sally frowned. 'Nobody's really sure,' she said. 'I...suffer from...hallucinations.'

Daisy looked puzzled. 'What's "halloo..."?'

'It means I see things that aren't there. And I hear things too, sometimes. Voices and so forth. Not all the time, of course. It comes and goes.'

'What do the doctors say?' asked Peter.

'Oh, Daddy won't let them see me any more.'

'Really?' This seemed ridiculous to Peter. Whenever he was ill, his mother always took him straight to a doctor.

'He says they don't know anything. He says they're all quacks.'

'Like ducks?' asked Daisy.

Sally smiled. 'I suppose so. I'm not quite sure what it means. I *did* go to see doctors at first, but they came up with all these silly ideas about what might be wrong with me, and Daddy got angry and said he wasn't going to waste any more money on them. They didn't really have a clue what was wrong.'

'It's sort of like *Heidi*, isn't it?' said Daisy brightly.

Sally stared at her. 'Is it?' she asked.

'Yes. You're like her friend, Clara. She can't walk, not until she goes and stays with Heidi's grandfather. Then the goat's milk and the mountain air make her well again.' She thought for a moment. 'Have you tried goat's milk?'

'We've tried everything,' said Sally. 'But nothing seems to work.'

'You won't be getting any fresh air,' observed Peter, pointing at the boarded-up window. 'Not with that thing there.'

'That's because the air isn't good for me,' said Sally bafflingly. 'They put that screen in to stop me from catching a chill.'

Peter frowned. That didn't seem to make any sense. 'I always thought that fresh air was good for you,' he said.

'It's not good for *me*,' said Sally. 'I'm too delicate. That's what Mrs Beesley always says.'

Daisy still wanted to talk about *Heidi*. 'Mrs Beesley is a bit like the woman in the book,' she observed, gleefully. 'What was her name again? Frau something?'

'Fraulein Rottenmeir!' said Sally delightedly, and they all sniggered.

'And Heidi's friend is even called Peter!' added Daisy excitedly. 'So you see, it really *is* just like the book!'

'Oh, yes,' chuckled Sally. 'I see what you mean.' Then her smile faded and a wistful look replaced it. 'If only life was like fiction,' she said. 'But I think it will take more than goat's milk and mountain air to get me out of this room.' She looked at Peter. 'So, tell me all about London,' she said. 'Or "Lunnen", as Mrs Beesley calls it. What's it like? I expect you go to the theatre every night, don't you?'

Peter shook his head. 'We *never* go to the theatre,' he said. He thought for a moment. 'We went to a pantomime last Christmas.'

'*Puss In Boots*,' said Daisy. 'There was a cat that could talk – but it was just a man dressed up, really. It was funny though. He kept asking us where things were and we'd shout, "It's behind you!" but by the time he'd turned round, it was always gone!'

'And the leading man was a woman dressed up,' added Peter, 'but she was called the Principal Boy, which I didn't really understand. She kept slapping her thigh and saying "Off we go!" and the cat had to sort out all her problems.'

'It sounds like fun,' said Sally. 'But…what about *real* theatre? And…the ballet?'

'We live in Dagenham,' said Peter. 'It's Essex, really.' That seemed to explain everything.

'I'd love to go to London,' said Sally. 'There's so much to see there. Big Ben, the Houses of Parliament...'

Peter and Daisy exchanged embarrassed looks. They *lived* so close to central London and hadn't been to see either of those things. There was an awkward silence and Peter gazed around the room, trying to find something else to talk about. His gaze fell on the cabinet beside Sally's bed, which contained a glass of water, a bottle of what must have been medicine and an open box containing two little lozenge-shaped objects. 'What are they?' he asked, pointing.

Sally glanced down at them. 'Oh, they're just my beeswax earplugs,' she said.

'Earplugs?' said Daisy. 'My friend Doreen wears those when she goes swimming. You don't go swimming, do you, Sally?'

'No, I don't. I don't go anywhere.' For a moment she looked exasperated. 'I wear the earplugs at night, so I can try to get some sleep.'

Peter was intrigued. 'Why can't you sleep without them?' he asked.

Sally looked unsure. 'There are noises at night. Owls hooting and so forth, the wind blowing...'

'And music,' added Daisy. She cast a guilty glance towards

the bedroom door, as though afraid that Mrs Beesley might be listening in. 'There was music last night,' she whispered. Peter could see that she wanted to say more, to mention the children she thought she'd seen in the garden, but she was holding back.

Sally looked troubled. 'There *is* music, sometimes. Daddy says it's just people in town, rehearsing for a concert.'

'In *town*?' Peter looked at her doubtfully. 'But that must be miles away.'

'Yes, but Daddy says with the land being so flat, you see, the sound of it carries on the wind. It can travel for long distances.' She sounded defensive, Peter thought, as though she didn't quite believe it herself. 'Especially at night, that's what Daddy says. So we got the earplugs, but sometimes I can *still* hear the music, even when I'm wearing them, and those nights I don't really get much sleep at all.'

'Don't put the earplugs in when I'm reading to you,' said Daisy sternly, and Sally smiled.

'I won't,' she promised. 'Are you a good reader, Daisy?'

'I'm the best in my class. I won a book prize for it.' Peter knew that she was very proud of this achievement and took every opportunity to tell people about it. She thought for a moment and then added, 'Maybe the film of *Heidi* will come to a cinema near here and we'll put you in a wheelchair and take you to see it.'

Sally smiled but she shook her head. 'I don't think that will ever happen. There's a cinema in Hythe but Daddy doesn't like me going out at night.'

'We could go to a matinee, couldn't we, Peter?'

'Yes, why not?' Peter smiled. He had another question to ask, but didn't feel he could speak quite as bluntly as Daisy would. 'Sally, I hope you don't mind me asking...but... what about your mother? Mr Sheldon said that something had happened to her, but he didn't say exactly what it was.'

'I...I'm afraid she's gone,' said Sally.

'Gone where?' cried Daisy, misunderstanding.

'I mean...she died, Daisy.'

'Oh no.' Daisy didn't seem to know what to say to that.

'Was it a long time ago?' asked Peter awkwardly.

'Oh yes, it was when I was just a toddler. A horse-riding accident, Daddy says. I've only ever seen her in old photographs. Daddy says she was a handsome woman with flaming red hair.' Sally smiled. 'I always think she sounds like a character out of a book.'

'I would hate it if my mummy died,' said Daisy.

There was another silence, this one so uncomfortable that

Peter was almost relieved when the door opened and Mrs Beesley stuck her cross-looking face into the room. 'Peter? Adam is ready for you now. Come along and leave the girls to their chatter.'

'Yes, Mrs Beesley.' Peter looked at Daisy. 'Will you be all right if I go?'

'Of course,' said Daisy scornfully, but he knew she was just trying to seem grown up in front of Sally.

'All right then,' he said. 'I'll see you later.' He followed Mrs Beesley out onto the landing and back down the stairs.

CHAPTER TWELVE

Following Mrs Beesley's instructions, Peter soon found Adam in the stables round the back of the house. He was rubbing thick yellow ointment into the scars on Bessie's flanks. As Peter strolled in, he glanced up guiltily and then looked away again.

'How is she?' asked Peter awkwardly.

'Oh, she's all right. It looks a lot worse than it is.' Adam sounded like he was trying to convince himself as much as Peter. 'I know the little girl was upset, but these 'orses is tough, they can take a bit of punishment. But Mrs B can be a bit too 'andy with that whip, sometimes.' He shook his head.

Peter stood there, feeling slightly embarrassed. 'She said you might have a few jobs for me,' he said.

'Did she now?' Adam scowled. 'That one's altogether too fond of finding work for idle hands,' he muttered. He looked at Peter doubtfully. 'So, you're gonna be my baily-boy, are you?'

'What's a baily-boy?' asked Peter.

'It's just a local expression. My assistant, I suppose is what you'd call it in the big city. How are you with a spade?'

'I've made sandcastles on Southend beach,' said Peter.

Adam sniggered. 'Southend beach!' he echoed. 'Bless my soul. You're a right joker, ain'tcha?'

'If you say so,' said Peter. He looked around the barn and noticed, through an open doorway, what looked like a small room with a cast-iron bed frame and a rickety pine dresser. A small metal stove in the corner looked like the only source of heat. He remembered something that Mrs Beesley had said about Adam, that he was just a hired hand. 'So you . . . *live* out here?' he said incredulously.

'That I do,' said Adam. 'It ain't much, but it suits me fine.'

Peter frowned. 'But the Grange is *huge*. Surely there must be a room there you could . . . ?'

'I likes to be out 'ere,' said Adam, a little too quickly. 'It's a space of my own and I can keep an eye on the animals. Sometimes I think animals is better company than human beings. You don't see animals being cruel to each other, do you? But people now, they can do terrible things. Despicable things.'

Peter didn't quite know what to say to this.

Adam clapped his dirty hands together and looked around, as though trying to think of something that Peter could do. 'Well, let's have a look,' he said. 'What could a young lad like yourself be handy for? Well, for starters, you can grab that shovel over there and help me to muck out Bessie's stall.'

'Muck...out?' murmured Peter. 'I'm not sure...'

'For Lord's sake, boy, you know what mucking out is, surely?' He looked at Peter's blank expression for a moment, then went on. 'We takes a couple of shovels and we dig out all that muck in there.' He pointed into Bessie's stall. 'We tip it into that wheelbarrow there...' He pointed again. '...and then we wheel it outside and heap it on the ruddy big pile out in the yard. Once we've done that, we get some fresh straw from those bales over there' – he pointed again – 'and we fill the stall with it. Couldn't be easier.'

Peter nodded. 'All right,' he said, eager to help. He thought for a moment. 'But...why?' he added.

'Why?' Adam looked at him incredulously. 'What do you mean, "why?"'

'Well...why take straw out if you're just going to put a load more back in?'

'Because it's dirty, innit? Not to put too fine a point on it, Bessie has gone and made a mess of what's already in there, so she needs clean straw, don't she? Lord, it's not that difficult to work out. I thought you was Mr Clever Clogs!'

Peter nodded. He fetched one of the shovels and then went to stand in the entrance of the stall. He wrinkled his nose. 'It smells terrible in here,' he observed.

'Nah. Good 'ealthy smell, that is. You sniff that up, boy, you sniff it up good. Do that and you'll come to no 'arm.'

Peter frowned. 'Do you have any gloves?' he asked.

'Gloves, he says!' Adam shook his head, as though he'd never heard anything so ridiculous in his life. 'What you want them for?'

'It looks dirty in here,' said Peter.

'Dirty, he says! That ain't dirt, boy. I've 'ad me 'ands in that stuff since I was a nipper and I've never 'ad a sick day in me life. Not one.' He reached into the pocket of his coat, took out a metal flask and uncorked it. He had a crafty glance over his shoulder before he raised it to his lips and took a gulp from its contents. Then he returned it to his pocket.

'What was that?' asked Peter.

'Medicine,' said Adam.

'But you just said you never got sick!'

'Never mind what I said, you get muckin' out!' Adam left Bessie and went to fetch the wheelbarrow for Peter. 'There, that's where you want to put it. Fill that up with straw. Now, off you go, let's see 'ow good you are.'

Peter swung the spade into the thick mixture of straw and dung, the motion stirring up an even worse smell than before. He tried not to gag as he transferred the first spadeful to the barrow.

'That's the ticket,' said Adam. 'Just keep at that until it's all gone. Couldn't be easier.' He found a spade for himself and came and stood beside Peter. 'Now,' he said, 'we'll take it in turns. A shovel each until the barrow is full.' He showed Peter how to do it, swinging his spade deep into the straw and lifting it into the barrow. Peter followed suit and pretty soon they'd established a rhythm between them. In a matter of minutes, the barrow was heaped with dirty straw.

'Excellent,' said Adam. 'We'll make a farm worker of you yet. Now, wheel that load out to the back of the yard and dump it on the heap. Then come back for more.'

Peter did as he was told. He pushed the barrow out into

the yard and round the back of the stables where he soon found a huge pile of used straw, stinking in the sunshine. Thousands of shiny black bluebottles buzzed and swooped around it, as though it was some kind of treasure. He found that he was enjoying this simple exercise, which for the moment at least, allowed him to push all his worries to the back of his mind. He upended the barrow against the base of the pile, the action stirring the flies into restless movement, the concerted buzz of them filling his head. He turned and looked across the yard to the house, which seemed to shimmer like a mirage in the morning sunlight. In the daytime, it seemed a much less forbidding place than it did at night. He hoped that Daisy was getting on all right with Miss Sally. It would be good for her to have a friend right now. He thought for a moment about the little house back in Dagenham and he wondered what his mother was doing. He wondered too what Mrs Beesley had done with that postcard. He made a mental note to ask her about it the next time he saw her.

When he got back to the barn with the empty barrow, Adam was sitting on a pile of filled sacks, smoking a cigarette and staring down at his scuffed old boots, as though trying to puzzle something out. Peter went back to the stall and recommenced work. 'It's a terrible thing, isn't it?' he said at last.

Adam looked up at him. 'What is?' he muttered.

'Miss Sally being ill, not being able to go anywhere.'

Adam studied him warily as he replied. 'Yeah, bad enough,' he said. 'What d'you know about it?'

'Only what she told me. That she has this...illness.' He glanced at Adam. 'What do you suppose is wrong with her?'

Adam shrugged his big shoulders. 'Blessed if I know,' he said. 'I ain't no doctor. Maybe it's just this place.'

Peter frowned. 'You mean the house?'

Adam shook his head. 'The Marsh. The whole area. It's...addled.'

'What do you mean? What's wrong with it?'

Adam shrugged. 'I'm only sayin' ...some people have got strange notions about the Marshes. They hear things. They *see* things.'

'What sort of things?'

'Ah well, that would depend on how long you've got. There's stories about these marshes that goes back for generations. Some people will tell you it's one of the most haunted places that ever there was.'

'What, you mean ghosts?'

'That's what some people calls 'em. And others reckon they's a natural part of the Marsh, as natural as the grass and the water. Why, I could tell you stories of—' Adam broke off as a shadow fell across him. They both looked up and saw that Mrs Beesley's tall figure was standing in the entrance to the barn. Peter noticed how Adam got quickly to his feet and made as if to lift one of the sacks that he'd been sitting on.

Mrs Beesley fixed him with a glare. 'What stories would they be, I wonder?' she asked, and Adam seemed unable to meet her gaze. He made a pathetic attempt to lift the sack to his shoulder, but it must have been heavier than he thought because he lowered it again, with a grunt, and dropped it back onto the heap.

'I was just telling the lad a few things about the Marsh.'

'What about it?' growled Mrs Beesley.

'I was just sayin' that some people 'ave odd stories about it,' stammered Adam. 'You know, things like—'

'You 'aven't got time for idle tittle-tattle,' she told him. She stepped into the barn and held out two grey canvas knapsacks. 'I bought the pair of you some bait for later on,' she said.

'Bait?' Peter was puzzled. 'Are we going to be trying to catch something?'

Adam grinned, showing nicotine-stained teeth. 'Bait is just a local word for grub,' he explained. 'We'll be eatin' our lunch on the hoof, see. Thanks, Mrs B!' He went to take the knapsacks from her but she held onto them for a moment and fixed her eyes on his.

'Least said, soonest mended,' she muttered. Then she released her hold on the knapsacks. She aimed one of her fake-looking grins in Peter's direction. 'I 'ope Adam isn't working you too hard,' she said.

'Umm.' Peter looked down at the mixture of hay and dung at his feet. 'No, I'm fine,' he said. 'Is Daisy all right?'

'Her and Miss Sally are gettin' on like an 'ouse on fire,' she assured him. 'They'll be thick as thieves afore you know it. You'll 'ave your nose put right out.' She smiled as though enjoying the idea.

'I wanted to ask you about the postcard.'

She looked at him. 'What about it? I filled in the address, didn't I? Gave it back to you, like you asked.'

'Yes, and...me and Daisy wrote a message to Mum, but...it's still on the hall table, where we left it. It should have been posted by now.'

'Don't you worry about that. You and Adam will be going into Hythe in a few days' time...'

114

'Will we?' asked Adam, who seemed puzzled by the remark.

'Yes. You will.' Mrs Beesley fixed him with a stern look, before turning back to look at Peter. 'So you can sort it then,' she said. 'Let your parents know what a lovely time you're having out here on the Marsh.'

'I just think . . .'

'Yes?'

'I just think they'll be worried if they don't hear from us soon. We don't have a telephone at home or anything, so . . .'

'Be patient. We'll sort it all out in good time,' she assured him. She turned to leave but not before throwing another quick glance in Adam's direction. 'Keep the lad occupied,' she told him, and then she strode out of the barn.

Adam glared after her for a moment, and Peter got the distinct impression that he didn't like Mrs Beesley very much, but that he was also, in some way, afraid of her. There was a silence, broken only by the sound of a cow lowing from somewhere nearby.

Adam looked at Peter and then gestured towards the stall. 'Well, come on,' he said, 'we'd better get on with it.' He picked up the other shovel and came over to join him and, working together, they filled the wheelbarrow again.

PART TWO

INTERMEZZO

CHAPTER THIRTEEN

Grandad Peter stops talking again. Helen realises she has been listening intently to his story, so intently that she has lost all sense of place and time. She is vaguely surprised to find that she is sitting in his room in the rest home, leaning forward in the rocking chair, her hands clenched at her sides. Outside, it has started to rain. She can hear the steady rhythm of it pattering against the window. She looks out into the garden and notes the way the winds are blowing the trees, making them lean to one side. It's a foul afternoon and she'll have to cycle home in this. But she's not ready to leave yet.

Grandad turns his head to look at her. 'Is this making any sense to you?' he asks her.

'Yes, of course,' she assures him. 'But...how come you've never told me any of it before?'

He sighs and shakes his head. 'For a long time I wanted

to forget all about it. I wanted to forget every detail. I suppose I just blotted it out of my mind. It's only lately that it's all started coming back to me.' He gazes around the cheerless little room that is now his world. 'I think, since Emily died, I've had a lot more time to reflect on things. I…well, I suppose I've been lonely. Sitting here, hour after hour, a man starts thinking about the past. About all the things that have happened to him. All the things he's done wrong…'

'You haven't done anything wrong, Grandad,' says Helen.

'We've all done things we regret,' he tells her. 'When you get to my age, you look back on them and you tremble.'

Helen suddenly feels uncomfortable. She gets up from her seat and goes over to the kitchen area. 'I'll make us some tea,' she suggests. She checks that the kettle is full and hits the 'on' switch.

Grandad Peter studies her for a moment. 'You're still intent on going on this…school trip?' He says the last two words as though they're some kind of curse.

Helen frowns. 'I don't know. My name's down for it. Mum's paid the deposit…And most of my friends are going. I usually go along with what they want to do.'

'You can't be like that about it, Helen. You need to stand up for yourself.'

Helen is slightly annoyed by this sudden change of direction. She wants him to go on with the story, she's gripped by his tale – but he seems determined on making his point. 'Take it from me, Helen, the Marsh is like nowhere else you've ever visited. Some places you go and you just know, deep inside, that something isn't right. That something evil exists there and has done for generations.'

She sighs. 'I don't suppose I'd be going to the exact same place,' she reasons. 'I mean, what would be the chances of that?'

'But perhaps it's nothing to do with chance,' he tells her. 'Perhaps it's fate.' He gazes at her. 'Sometimes, things are just meant to be and we have no control over them.' He watches as she busies herself making two cups of tea. 'I bet you didn't expect to spend your afternoon like this,' he mutters. 'Listening to an old man's ramblings.'

'Don't be silly. It's an incredible story. Really creepy.' She brings over the teas and sets one down beside him on the small table. Then she settles back into the rocking chair and sips at her own drink.

'So you believe me? You don't think I've gone batty?'

'Course not.' She thinks for a moment. 'The music though...that's so weird. Could there have been some reason for it? You know, like Sally's father said, maybe a band practising nearby...or...or maybe somebody just playing the same record over and over.' She thought for a moment. 'You did have records then, I suppose?'

Grandad Peter smiles ruefully. 'We had gramophone records,' he said. 'But...this wasn't a recording. I knew that much.'

'And how come nobody else noticed it?'

'Because only the children could hear it,' said Grandad Peter. 'On that first night, I thought that Mrs Beesley and Adam were just pretending that they couldn't. But later on, I understood that the adults didn't hear the music simply because it wasn't intended for them. It was only for the children.' He lifted his own mug and sipped at its contents.

'The days slipped by,' he said. 'On the third day we were there, war was declared. We heard Neville Chamberlain announcing it on the wireless and we knew then that there could be no avoiding it. The war would change everything that we knew. But out on the Marsh, we seemed so detached from it...so remote. It was as if it was all happening in an entirely different world.' He set down his mug. 'Almost *before we knew it, we'd been there nearly a week. I worked around the farm with Adam. I got to like him, respect him. There was a good soul lurking behind that gruff exterior. But I could also tell that he was hiding something from me...and that he was conflicted about it. He wanted to warn me, I think, but he was too scared of Mrs Beesley and too devoted to Mr Sheldon to go against them. So he took solace in whisky. Most nights he was too drunk to do anything more than sleep.'*

'And...Daisy?' prompted Helen.

'Daisy developed her friendship with Sally. They made good companions. They both loved reading and...they both heard things.'

'The music?'

He nodded. 'Oh, I heard it too, most nights. Faint, but always in the background. It was different for Daisy. I could see that something in the music had gripped her. She seemed to grow paler by the day, with dark rings around her eyes. She had a haunted look. And more than once, I caught her whispering to that damned doll...'

'You must have been scared.'

'Not in the daytime. When the sun shone, the Grange seemed agreeable enough. But at night, everything changed.

The place had an eerie quality to it. Unnerving...sometimes terrifying. And I began to ask myself, was I imagining things? Or was something at work, just out of reach, just on the other side of a paper-thin veil? Trying to exert a hold on the Grange. On Daisy. On me. Growing stronger, night by night...'

CHAPTER FOURTEEN

Peter woke in terror once again. He lay there, waiting for his breath to settle to a more normal rhythm, while he gazed around the attic room. The same dream, the one about the canal, the wolf and that hideous face rising up out of the water...

He sat up suddenly as an already familiar sound came to his ears: the sound of a flute playing *that* tune. He'd heard it every night he'd been here, but it sounded much closer now, he thought, as though the musician was somewhere nearby, maybe just outside the house. And then a terrible conviction took hold of him, the idea that Daisy was in some kind of trouble. Perhaps it was simply the awful dream that had spooked him and yet, he felt with a nagging certainty that whatever that music was, it was something bad. And he remembered the faraway look on Daisy's face the first time she'd heard it. When she'd said how much she liked it...

He groped around in the dark until he found the matches, and after a couple of unsuccessful attempts he managed to get the candle alight. He took up the holder, threw aside the covers and headed for the door, wincing at every creak of the floorboards beneath his bare feet. He unlatched the door and peeped out onto the top landing, which looked decidedly forbidding in the uncertain light of the guttering candle. He walked slowly towards the stairs, keeping the flat of one hand in front of the flame, terrified of it being blown out and finding himself standing in total darkness. Only now did it occur to him that it would have been wiser to put the box of matches into his pyjama pocket and he thought about going back for it, but the sense of foreboding in him deepened, so he started down the rickety stairs, placing one foot in front of the other as quietly as he could manage.

He reached the first-floor landing and angled round to start along it. He stopped to listen for a moment. In one of the rooms on this floor, somebody was snoring, a low, rumbling sound that seemed to resonate on the air. Mr Sheldon, perhaps? Outside, that infernal music continued to play, repeating the same phrase over and over again, with a maddening intensity. Then he heard the other sound. The rattling of metal against metal, as though somebody was shaking a length of chain and now he was sure that it was coming from Miss Sally's room. But he stopped at Daisy's door. He lifted an arm to grasp the handle and turned it. The door creaked slowly open.

The cold hit him instantly. He was aware of his breath clouding as it left his mouth. Why was it so cold in the room? The rest of the house didn't feel like this.

He stood in the doorway, looking around, horribly aware of the flame of the candle he was holding reflecting in scores of watching glass eyes. The dolls. Then he noticed that the huge bed in the centre of the room was empty and his heart skipped a beat; but almost instantly he relaxed when he saw Daisy kneeling up on the window ledge, staring intently out into the night. The window was open, the night air stirring her hair, but she seemed oblivious to it. Peter entered the room and closed the door behind him. He set down his candle on a table and turned back to Daisy. Now he saw to his surprise that so engrossed was she with whatever it was she was looking at, she seemed to be unaware that she was crushing a couple of Sally's valuable dolls beneath her knees.

'Daisy?' whispered Peter. 'What are you doing out of bed?'

She didn't seem to hear him. She kept her gaze fixed on whatever it was that had caught her attention. He took a step closer and spoke louder.

'Daisy?'

Now she turned to look at him and he felt his sense of unease deepen as he saw that she had a look of excited bliss on her face. She was smiling serenely at him.

'Peter,' she said, in that same dreamy tone he remembered from before. 'Come and look. They're here again.'

'Who?' he asked, but he knew even before he walked across to the window what he was going to see out there. And still he tried to reason with her. 'At this time of night? You...you must be mistaken.' He moved closer. 'Daisy! Wake up!'

She seemed to snap out of her dreamlike state, but she stayed where she was at the window, staring down at something he couldn't yet see. 'Come and look!' she repeated triumphantly and pointed. Peter followed the line of her finger.

He felt a cold chill shudder through him, because she was right, she'd been right all along, he could see them out in the mist-shrouded garden, three ragged figures, all girls. They were quite a way off and they appeared to be dancing, dancing to that tune. And now that he thought about it, the music was louder than ever. The girls had their arms up and their heads back and they were lurching joyfully around to the sound, as though transported by it. There was something about their gangling arms and legs that didn't seem quite right, but they were too distant for him to make out much detail. And then, further off, at the top of the garden, Peter caught a glimpse of another figure, a man, perhaps, though in the mist it was hard to be sure. His arms were up in front of him and something in his hands glinted in the moonlight, but even as Peter registered this, the figure began to move away, heading along an avenue of shrubs at the top of the garden, still playing his tune and the children wheeled around to follow him, dancing along in his wake, as though the music was summoning them, compelling them to follow.

'Let's go,' whispered Daisy. 'Let's go and dance with them!'

'No,' hissed Peter. 'We mustn't.' He didn't know exactly what was happening out there, but he knew in his heart that it wasn't something he wanted to be involved with, not for one moment.

'But it looks such *fun*!' cried Daisy.

'No it doesn't,' he told her. 'And you heard what Adam said. It's dangerous out there. There's water…'

'They look like they know where they're going,' observed Daisy. 'Come on, let's just join in for a minute. *Please.*'

He shook his head. He caught a last glimpse of the girls as they danced away into the mist. The music was finally diminishing in volume. Peter closed the window, then took Daisy's hand and helped her off the seat. As she stepped down, a couple of the dolls fell onto the floor.

She looked down at them in dismay. 'Did I do that?' she gasped. 'Mrs Beesley will be angry.'

'It'll be all right,' he assured her. He set down the candle for a moment and picking up the fallen dolls one-by-one, he sat them carefully back on the ledge where Daisy had been kneeling. None of them seemed to be damaged. 'What were you thinking?' he asked. 'You know they're worth a lot of money.'

'I don't know.' Daisy had the look of somebody who'd just woken from a deep sleep. 'I don't even remember getting out of bed,' she said. 'I think I was having a bad dream...'

You too? thought Peter, but he said nothing. 'Well, never mind about that, let's get you back into bed before you freeze to death.' He led her over to the big four-poster and saw that the small doll she'd been holding the other day was propped up against the pillows, gazing intently up at him. 'Where's Eva?' he asked.

'I threw her away,' said Daisy, as though it was of no account. 'She was broken anyway.'

Peter looked at her in disbelief. 'We could have tried mending her,' he said.

'Tillie told me not to bother.'

'Tillie? Who's Tillie?' he asked her, but somehow he already knew the answer, even before she pointed to the little doll on the bed. And he thought he remembered Mrs Beesley mentioning the name before. Wasn't that the doll that Miss Sally used to talk to?

'She's my new doll,' said Daisy.

'She's not your doll,' Peter reminded her. 'And besides, a doll can't tell you to do anything.'

Daisy gave him a smug look. 'That's what you think,' she said.

The expression on her face disturbed him. It was the look of someone who had a secret and wasn't prepared to share it.

'Why did you call her Tillie?' asked Peter. 'Did Mrs Beesley tell you to call her that?'

Daisy shook her head. 'I call her that because it's her name,' she said.

'Well, anyway, back into bed,' he told her, and he helped her to climb up onto it and settled her under the covers. He picked up Tillie, meaning to put her with the others on the window ledge, but Daisy grabbed his wrist and the strength in her little hand shocked and surprised him.

'Leave her here,' she said. It wasn't a request, more a command.

'I . . . I don't know what Mrs B will say if she catches you.'

'I don't care. I can't sleep without Tillie.'

He frowned. 'All right,' he said reluctantly. He replaced the doll against the pillow and made as if to leave, but Daisy still clung onto his wrist.

'Will you get in with us?' she asked. 'Just until we fall asleep.'

'I shouldn't really,' he told her, but he was pretty cold himself so, after a few moment's hesitation, he climbed in beside her and snuggled up tight. They lay there in silence for a while.

'Who were those children?' asked Daisy at last.

'I don't know,' said Peter. He kept thinking about the dream, that hideous white face bobbing up out of the water. And he had a horrible feeling that the two things were connected in some way that he couldn't yet see.

'I don't like it here,' said Daisy. 'I want to go home.'

'We can't,' Peter told her. 'I know it's hard, but we have to try and make the best of it. A new place always seems strange, but...'

'But it's not new any more,' said Daisy. 'We've been here for ages. And we still haven't sent that postcard home. Mummy will be worried.'

'I know. I keep asking about it. Mrs B says we'll be going to Hythe soon and I can post it then. But she's always putting it off.'

'I wish we could just post ourselves,' said Daisy.

Peter smiled. 'Wouldn't that be a whiz?' he said. 'But it'll be all right. You'll soon—' He broke off. He'd been about to tell her that they'd soon get used to the Grange, but somehow he couldn't bring himself to say such a thing about this odd house. There were secrets here, he thought, secrets that might be better left as secrets. But at the same time, he knew he'd do everything he could to find them out.

'Peter?'

'Yes?'

'Do you think that Mummy and Daddy are all right?'

'Yes,' he said. 'Of course they are.'

'And do you think we'll ever see them again?'

'Of course we will. It won't be long, you'll see.'

'And Peter, do you think...?' Her voice trailed away and her breathing settled into a slow, regular rhythm. But even so, he stayed where he was for a good half hour, wanting to be sure she wouldn't wake again, before he finally got out of bed and gathered up his candle.

He took a last look at Daisy. She was sleeping with Tillie clutched tight to her chest. The doll's face smiled out at Peter and he couldn't help but feel there was a triumphant expression in those green eyes. He told himself not to be silly. It was just a doll. He turned away, went to the door and made his way back up the stairs to his own room.

CHAPTER FIFTEEN

When they went down to breakfast the following morning, Mrs Beesley was in her usual place at the cooking range, but this morning she was stirring a big pan of lumpy grey porridge. Peter and Daisy took their places at the table and Peter studied the woman's back as she worked. He was determined to talk to her about what was going on here, but he waited until she came over to the table and set two large bowls down in front of them.

Daisy gazed down into her bowl without enthusiasm. She looked ill this morning, Peter thought, pale and drawn, her eyes ringed with grey. 'What's this?' she muttered.

'It's porridge!' exclaimed Mrs Beesley, exasperated. 'You must 'ave had porridge before, surely?'

'Not this colour,' said Daisy glumly. 'Mummy makes our porridge with evaporated milk.'

'Does she now?' Mrs Beesley slid a large pot of fruit jam

across the table. 'Shove a blob of that in it,' she suggested. 'It'll set you up a treat. You look like you could do with a good feed. Too finicky by half, you are.' She looked at Peter accusingly, as though daring him to complain, so he spooned a large helping of grey mush into his mouth and gulped it down. It tasted every bit as unappetising as it looked.

'You'll be wanting tea, I expect,' said Mrs Beesley and she started back towards the range.

'Who are the girls?' asked Peter, and she stopped in her tracks, but she didn't turn her head to look at him when she replied.

'What girls?' she asked, and she continued on her way to the range.

'The ones who were in the garden last night,' he said, and took another spoonful of porridge.

'I don't know what you're talkin' about,' she told him as she busied herself with the teapot.

Peter wasn't going to let it go. 'Daisy told you about them days ago,' he said. 'She saw them the first night we stayed here. Don't you remember?'

Mrs Beesley's large shoulders shrugged. 'I remember she said somethin' daft but I don't exactly recall what it was.'

'She told you she'd seen girls dancing in the garden. I

didn't believe her then, but last night I saw them too. They were out on the lawn. It must have been gone midnight.'

'I think somebody's been 'aving a dream,' said Mrs Beesley.

'We weren't dreaming,' said Daisy. 'The music woke me up, so I got out of bed to look. And then Peter came down and he saw them too. There were three of them.'

Now Mrs Beesley came back to the table, carrying the teapot.

'Children from Hythe, I expect. Larking about. You know what youngsters are like these days. No respect for nothin'. A good hidin' is what they need.'

Peter shook his head. 'They weren't larking about,' he insisted. 'They were *dancing*. A man with a flute was playing music for them, the same music I've heard every night since I've been here.'

'Music? Oh, that'll be the band in the village,' said Mrs Beesley. 'They often rehearse late into the night...'

Peter shook his head. 'I know that's what you tell Sally, but I don't believe it,' he said. 'Where is this village, anyway? I thought there was nothing for miles.'

Now Mrs Beesley looked cross. 'How dare you question me?' she said. 'I won't be challenged in my own house.'

'But the—'

'Enough, I say!' She slammed her hand down on the table top, hard enough to make Daisy drop her spoon. 'You two want to be grateful that Mr Sheldon has taken you in and he's feeding you and giving you a place to stay. And is this how you repay him? Coming up with these fanciful notions the whole time? Complaining about the food and making up daft stories... Well, I won't stand for it, do you hear? In my day, children were seen and not heard. Now be quiet and eat your breakfast.'

Peter continued to spoon porridge into his mouth, but Daisy's eyes filled with tears and her shoulders began to shake.

'Oh, now come along, there's no need for that,' said Mrs Beesley, suddenly all contrite. 'No need at all. I...I didn't mean to shout, honest I didn't.' She forced an unconvincing smile. 'Peter, you've got that postcard all ready for your mother, haven't you?'

He nodded suspiciously.

'Good. Because you and Adam are going out on the Marsh today, and after you've seen to the sheep and all that, he'll take you into Hythe, to the post office there and you'll be able to send it off to her. You'd like that, wouldn't you?'

Peter nodded. 'Of course,' he said.

'Well, that's all settled then. I'll make up some bait for the two of you and you can make a day of it. And Daisy and Miss Sally can have a lovely day all to themselves talkin' about whatever takes their fancy.' She went round to Daisy and used her pinafore to wipe the girl's tears away. 'Such a fuss over nothing,' she said. 'I didn't mean to shout, honest I didn't. I tell you what, Daisy, would you like something else instead of the porridge? Hmm? How about a nice slice of buttered bread? Would you like that?'

Daisy nodded and Mrs Beesley looked at Peter. 'You too, Peter. Bread?'

'All right,' he said. He couldn't help but feel suspicious, it wasn't like her to be so accommodating. He watched as she scurried back to the range to prepare the food, but he wasn't fooled by her good humour, not for one moment. She knew more than she was letting on and all this bluster was just her attempt to sweep things under the carpet. But, he told himself, Adam knew something too, and if the two of them were going to spend the day together, without the threat of Mrs Beesley turning up at any moment, then maybe he might find some answers to his questions.

CHAPTER SIXTEEN

Half an hour later, Peter and Adam set off across the Marsh, each of them carrying a knapsack across their shoulder with their 'bait' inside. They walked down the drive and out through the stone gateposts. Peter glanced back, hoping that Daisy would be all right. He couldn't help feeling that spending so much time with Sally was having an effect on Daisy, making her moody, quite unlike her usual self. But, he told himself, nothing bad was going to happen in the daylight.

Adam ignored the road, which stretched directly ahead of them, and instead angled right, where a dirt track led away across the land, unreeling like a length of brown ribbon for as far as the eye could see. The weather was pleasant enough, some hazy sunshine peeping through occasional clouds. There was no other sign of life around here. Peter could only assume that the sheep he'd heard so much about were a long way off, but he was glad to be getting away from the dark, shadowy confines of the Grange.

After walking for fifteen minutes or so, Peter became aware of something off to his left – a long line of trees and bushes running in a straight line across the land, more or less parallel to the track he was walking on. It was so unusual to see trees here, he couldn't help remarking on it. He also thought he noticed the shimmer of water, reflecting in the sunlight and he was reminded again of the nightmare he'd been having since he arrived here. 'What's over there?' he asked. 'A river?'

Adam barely looked up from the way ahead. He seemed preoccupied today, lost in his own thoughts. He grunted. 'Nah,' he said. 'It's just Lord Pitt's Ditch.' He paused, then shook his head. 'That's what folks call it in these parts, but it's properly called the Royal Military Canal. Sounds grand, dunnit? But a right useless thing it is. T'was dug hundreds of years ago and cost thousands and thousands of pounds, but it's never been no use to man nor beast.'

'There's somebody over there,' said Peter, pointing. 'Look.'

A man was standing near the edge of the water. He seemed to be studying it through a pair of binoculars. Then he glanced up, noticed Peter and Adam and waved a hand at them.

'Oh Lord 'elp us,' muttered Adam. 'It's Professor Know-All!'

The man was approaching them now, walking briskly. As he moved closer, Peter saw that he was an elderly fellow, dressed in a tweed jacket and plus-fours, with long plaid socks sticking up from heavy walking boots. He had a shapeless tweed hat crammed down onto his head and the few wisps of hair that stuck out from it were silvery-grey.

'That can't be his name,' reasoned Peter, under his breath.

'May as well be,' muttered Adam. 'Professor Lowell is his real name. Local historian. Thinks he knows more about this place than those of us who've lived here all our blessed lives.' There was bitter resentment in his voice. 'A right busybody, he is. Don't let him get you talking, we'll be 'ere all day.'

'Hello there, Adam,' called the professor, as he came up to them. 'Lovely day for it, what? Going out to tend your flock, I suppose?'

Adam nodded sullenly, but didn't reply.

'And who have we here? Bit of a new face, I think.' The professor had a hearty, cultured voice, which Peter recognised instantly. He'd heard it a week ago, when he'd been hiding under a blanket with Daisy in the back of Adam's cart. This was the man whom Mrs Beesley had lied to, when she claimed not to have seen any evacuees.

'This 'ere is Peter,' grunted Adam, with evident reluctance to speak. 'He's staying with us at the Grange for a bit.'

'Is that so?' The professor reached out and shook Peter's hand vigorously. Up close, he looked a hundred years old, his face lined and weather-beaten from exposure to the elements. 'You're a relative of the family, are you?'

'No, sir,' said Peter. 'I'm an evacuee,' he added, and was aware of Adam letting out a frustrated sigh beside him.

'Is that right?' The professor shot an accusing look at Adam, but didn't pursue the matter any further. 'So, you're from the Big Smoke, no doubt?'

'The . . . Big Smoke, sir?'

'London, of course! I'm from that part of the world myself. Taught history at King's College back in the day. Came out here on holiday thirty years ago and fell in love with the place. Never went back! Which particular bit of London do you hail from?'

'Dagenham, sir.'

'Ah, splendid, absolutely splendid! The beating heart of industry, eh? Where would our war effort be without Ford

Motors? That's what I'd like to know! So, you're going to be working with Adam, I suppose. A trainee Looker. Make sure he doesn't work you too hard. Here.' He reached into his pocket and pulled out a coin, which he then pressed into Peter's hand. 'There's a tanner for you, young feller. Make sure you don't spend it all at once!'

'Thank you, sir!' Peter was delighted. A sixpence was big money where he came from. Now the professor turned his attention to Adam. 'Heard the latest about the canal?' he asked.

Adam shook his head. 'I ain't 'eard nothin',' he said flatly.

'Seems the Army have their eye on it. Had a team of engineers down here only yesterday, carrying out a survey. Turns out they're planning to put concrete pillboxes all the way along it. Machine gun emplacements, I shouldn't wonder! They must have decided that what was built to keep out one dictator could work just as effectively with our Mr Hitler.' He tapped the side of his nose. 'Mind you, that's all hush-hush. Mum's the word, old boy!' He returned his attention to Peter. 'So, lad, how are you finding things at the Grange?'

'Umm . . . well . . .'

'I expect you've met Miss Sally. A proper little bookworm,

I seem to remember. Mind you, I haven't seen her in a very long time.'

'Well, that would be because she's ill,' said Peter.

'Ill?' The professor looked puzzled.

'Yes, sir. Well, she can't get out of bed. She reads even more, these days – her room is full of books.'

The professor looked quizzically at Adam. 'Since when has she been bedridden?' he asked. 'She certainly seemed fine when I saw her at the spring fair in April. She was running around, chasing the other—'

'We really should be goin',' interrupted Adam, grabbing Peter's arm and pulling him on along the track. 'Them sheep won't look after 'emselves.'

'Oh, that's all right, I'll walk along with you,' suggested the professor, failing to take the hint. 'Give me a chance to stretch the old pins, what?' He fell into step with them and they walked for a while in silence. The professor seemed to be thinking about something. 'So, what exactly is wrong with Miss Sally?' he asked.

'Nobody really knows,' Peter told him. 'She has hallucinations. She...sees things...and hears things.'

'Is that right? Well, I can't say I'm entirely surprised. I've told Arthur often enough that he needs to get her away from that place. But he never listens.' He gave Adam another long, meaningful look. 'You give her my best wishes,' he told Peter.

'I will, sir.'

'And how exactly are things at the Grange?' he asked.

'Umm. Good,' said Peter. He didn't think he could talk about the strange happenings that had been going on to a virtual stranger, especially with Adam there.

'Got quite a history, that place,' said the professor. 'Devoted a whole chapter to it in my book.'

'You've written a book?' cried Peter, impressed. He'd never met a writer before. He found himself wishing that Daisy was with him. He imagined how impressed she'd be when he told her.

'Well, just a modest volume of local history,' admitted the professor. 'Not exactly station bookstand material, you understand. But quite well received when it was first released.'

'Not everyone was so pleased with it,' muttered Adam under his breath; but if he heard, the professor paid no attention.

'And of course, there's plenty of stuff about the canal,' added the professor. 'A special area of interest for me. One might say, a bit of an obsession. To my mind, it's one of the greatest accomplishments of military history.'

Adam grunted. 'That's your opinion,' he said. 'And I expect you're entitled to it. Some other folks think it was a waste of time and money.'

The professor smiled. 'Not everyone,' he said calmly.

Peter wondered why Adam was being so rude to the old man – quite unlike the pleasant, good-natured fellow that he had come to know over the past week.

'Of course,' continued the professor, 'there's also a chapter in the book about the link between the canal and the Grange.'

'What link is that?' asked Peter, his curiosity aroused.

'You shouldn't be raking up stuff from the past,' Adam warned Professor Lowell. 'Some things are better left alone.'

'I disagree,' said the professor coldly. 'And I'm perfectly sure the boy would like to hear about it.' He looked down at Peter. 'Isn't that so, young man?'

Peter shrugged, uncomfortably. 'Er...I...don't mind,' he said. It was clear that there was some kind of bad feeling between Adam and the professor and it was hard to know what to do for the best. He felt torn between pleasing the stranger, who had given him money, and his ill-tempered host, who just seemed to want to shut the old man up.

'Good lad!' said the professor. 'But where to start? That's the question. Well, to tell the story properly, I have to take you all the way back to the early eighteen hundreds. At that time, the rise of Napoleon had given the powers-that-be the very real fear that we were open to invasion by sea. So some bright spark came up with the idea of making a natural defence here in the south of England.' He waved a hand in the general direction of the canal. 'In 1804, the first sod was dug out from the ground to form the Royal Military Canal and the work continued for the next four and a half years. As you can imagine, it was a monumental undertaking...'

'Waste of effort if you ask me,' grunted Adam, but again the professor ignored him.

'Something like one thousand, five hundred men were employed on the various stages of the work. Hereabouts, it was carried out by French prisoners of war. There were around twenty troops under the command of a certain Captain Jean Micheaux. He was—'

'That's enough,' snarled Adam. He stopped walking and turned back to confront the old man. 'We 'aven't got time to listen to this nonsense. You be about your business now.'

Peter was astonished by the change in Adam. He looked angry now, his eyes bulging, his hands bunched into fists.

The two men stood there glaring at each other in silence for a moment. Then the professor seemed to back down.

'Well, I can see you're not in the best mood for company today,' he said. 'So I'll leave you to it.' He nodded to Peter and began to turn away. Adam swung round and continued walking, but the professor, sensing an opportunity, reached quickly into his knapsack and pulled out a slim book. He pressed it into Peter's hands. 'Read it,' he whispered urgently. Peter took the book and, glancing guiltily at Adam's back, he slipped it into his own knapsack.

He got it hidden away just in time. Adam paused and looked back at the professor. 'Are you going or what?' he asked bluntly.

'Of course, I'm going. Good day to you, Adam. Hopefully I'll find you in a better mood next time we meet.' He began to walk away, but hesitated when another thought seemed to cross his mind. He turned and looked enquiringly at Peter. 'Tell me, lad,' he said. 'Are you here on your own?'

Peter shook his head. 'No, sir, my sister Daisy's with me.'

The professor's mouth fell open. He looked as though something terrible had just occurred to him. 'How old is your sister?' he gasped.

But then Adam came marching back again, his face

contorted with anger. 'Enough!' he roared, and he raised an arm as though to hit the professor, prompting the old man to take a couple of steps backwards. 'You be on your way now, or I won't be responsible for my actions.'

'But . . . Adam, you can't . . .'

'Be gone!' This time, Adam actually threw out an arm and pushed the professor hard in the chest, nearly sending the old man sprawling. Then he grabbed Peter's wrist and dragged him on along the path. The professor made no attempt to follow, but he shouted after them.

'Peter, you keep a close eye on your sister, do you hear me? Don't let her out alone, especially at night. It's not safe.'

Peter looked back over his shoulder, but Adam was too strong to resist. The professor was standing there, his expression grim. He shouted something else, but Peter couldn't quite make out what he was saying. He looked up at Adam.

'Why did you push him like that?' he gasped.

'Because he's mad,' grunted Adam. 'Away with the blummin' fairies. He's written a load of nonsense in that book of his and he's started to believe it.'

'But . . . something strange *is* going on here,' insisted Peter. 'You must know that. I've heard music! A flute playing. You say you can't hear it, but I can and I know I'm not imagining it.'

Adam stared straight at him. 'I ain't never heard nothin' like that,' he said. 'Not never.'

'But I'm not making it up! And... last night, there were girls dancing in the garden. Dancing to the music in the middle of the night.'

'What if there was?' snapped Adam. He laughed derisively. 'I told you strange things go on around here, didn't I?' He looked intently at Peter. 'But dancing girls is one thing,' he said. He jerked a thumb over his shoulder in the direction the professor had taken. 'What he talks about, that's another.'

'I don't understand.'

'You don't need to understand,' Adam assured him. 'The Marsh does as the Marsh thinks fit. You and me, we just 'ave to get on the best we can.' He was striding onwards, his gaze fixed on the way ahead. The stern expression on his face suggested that he did not want to discuss the matter any further. He raised an arm and pointed.

Now Peter could see up ahead of them the distant white blobs of a large flock of sheep spread out across the far horizon. He glanced back again and saw that the professor had turned away and was trudging dejectedly back in the direction of the canal. Peter didn't know the old man, but he was sure of one thing. He wasn't mad. And he had warned Peter that Daisy was in danger. Before he left home, Peter had promised his mother that he wouldn't let anything bad happen to his little sister. He knew in that moment that he would do whatever it took to protect her. No matter what the cost.

CHAPTER SEVENTEEN

Now they had finally found the sheep, Peter couldn't help wondering why they had bothered. The creatures stood around, baahing and munching grass, great woolly lumps with stupid faces and crescent-shaped black nostrils. There must have been a couple of hundred of them, ranged across the landscape, pretty much as far as the eye could see. They took little notice of the two humans who had travelled such a long way to find them.

'What do we do now?' asked Peter.

'Do?' Adam gave him a look. 'Well, we checks 'em over, don't we? We makes sure none of 'em 'as any problems.'

He began to stride through the midst of his flock and they parted on either side of him, like two woolly waves dividing to admit a latter-day Moses.

Peter trudged grimly along in his wake. 'How often do you have to do this?' he asked.

'Once a week, sometimes twice. And every day in the lambing season. You see, sheep ain't the cleverest of creatures. You've got to keep an eye on 'em. Otherwise, they'll just follow along.'

Peter frowned, puzzled. 'I don't know what you mean,' he said.

'Well, I remember one time, there was this one sheep, she'd come to this place where the ground dropped away sharpish like. Sort of like a little cliff, it were, some ten or twelve foot high.' He seemed in a better mood now he was on his favourite subject, Peter noticed. Adam looked around at the flat landscape and shook his head. 'Lord even knows how she managed to find the one place in these parts where such a thing could 'appen, but sure enough, she did. Walked right over the edge of the drop and fell onto the rocks below.' He shook his head. 'Killed, she was. Stone dead.' He sighed, remembering. 'Well, that would have been bad enough on its own, but of course there was a whole load of other sheep following her, wasn't there? You'd think they have the sense to see what had happened and back off, but no. Walked over the drop, one by one, they did. By the time it dawned on 'em, that it was a bad thing to do, must 'ave been a dozen of 'em had fallen, one on top of t'other. When I got there, it weren't a pretty sight. They wasn't all dead, mind, but the ones that had survived had broken their legs and all sorts. I 'ad to put 'em out of their misery.'

Peter grimaced. 'How did you do that?' he asked.

'Never you mind how I did it,' Adam told him. 'Let's just say, I made it quick and easy for 'em and leave it at that. But that's the kind of thing you 'ave to be prepared to do when you're a Looker. It ain't for the faint-hearted, I'll tell you that much.'

'Will *we* have to kill sheep?' asked Peter, apprehensively.

'Hopefully not.' Adam gestured ahead of him. 'We'll head up to Thursby Lake now. Sometimes I 'as to pull drowned sheep out of that. That ain't no picnic, when it 'appens.'

They continued walking through the massive flock. Peter found he couldn't concentrate on the task at hand. He kept thinking about what the professor had said about Daisy. How she was in danger. Part of him wanted to turn round and run all the way back to the Grange, but he doubted that he'd be able to find his way there without Adam's help.

'When are we heading back?' he asked.

Adam shrugged. 'What's the big 'urry?' he asked.

'I just wondered.'

'We'll be ready when we're ready and not before.'

'But we *will* be there before nightfall, won't we? I mean, it's not safe to be out after dark, is it? Even you and Mrs B said that when we first arrived.'

'Well, of course not. You can have accidents in the dark, go off the road and blunder into a bog.'

'And it's not because of anything else? Like...ghosts.'

Adam snorted. 'There you go again. That's what you get for listening to the mad professor. He's enough to give anyone the creeps.'

'He seemed clever enough to me,' said Peter.

'Don't you be fooled. He's like all toffs. Thinks 'is la-di-da accent will let him away with whatever nonsense is in 'is head. But puttin' somethin' down in print don't make it the truth. You'd do well to remember that, boy.'

'You said yourself that lots of people think the Marsh is haunted.'

'Aye, I said that and maybe it's true.'

'Well, then—'

'Shush boy! I can't even think with all your prattling!'

They reached the lake a little after midday. It looked inviting in the sunshine, the wide stretch of olive-green water surrounded by trees and rushes. Adam and Peter made their way slowly to the water's edge, then worked their way around it in a slow circle, checking the shallows for any problems. Sheep were grazing nearby, but none of them seemed to have got themselves into trouble. It took them the best part of an hour to complete the circuit, but when they had come back to their starting point, Adam found a spot a short distance from the water's edge and indicated to Peter that they should sit down.

'We may as well 'ave our bait here,' he said. He took off his overcoat and threw it down onto the grass, to act as a kind of blanket. He settled himself down on it and Peter sat beside him. He unslung his knapsack and took out his packed lunch, making sure that Adam didn't get a glimpse of the book that the professor had given him. He was eager to have a look at it, but supposed he would have to wait for the right opportunity. Adam was hardly likely to sit there and let him read it. He unwrapped the brown paper parcel that Mrs Beesley had prepared for him to find a chunk of fresh baked bread, a bottle of water and a couple of slices of ham. He began to eat eagerly but noticed that Adam was rolling a cigarette and staring thoughtfully off across the lake.

'Aren't you eating?' Peter asked him. 'Mrs B's made us a good lunch.'

'Ain't got no appetite for anything that woman does these days,' muttered Adam. He finished making the cigarette, reached into his pocket for a box of matches and lit up. He blew out a fragrant cloud of smoke. Then he placed his knapsack down as a pillow and, lying back, rested his head on it. He lay there, gazing at the sky, smoking his cigarette. 'Trouble with her is, she makes these plans and people like me are just expected to go along with 'em. Don't matter what we think about it.' He reached into the pocket of his waistcoat and pulled out a silver flask. He uncorked it and took a generous swig.

'Still on the medicine, I see,' said Peter.

'Aye. Keeps the flu away,' said Adam.

'Why do you drink so much, Adam?'

'That's none of your business.'

'My father had a friend who was always drinking. And when Dad asked him why, he'd say he was drinking to forget. Are you trying to forget about something?'

'Maybe.' Adam blew out a great cloud of smoke.

'What is it?' asked Peter.

There was a pause. Then Adam said, 'I dunno, I've forgotten.' He sniggered at his own poor joke, but Peter wasn't going to be distracted so easily.

'Why did you make me and Daisy hide?' he asked.

Adam turned his head to look at him. 'What you on about?' he muttered.

'The day we arrived, when we were in the horse and cart with you and Mrs Beesley. We met Professor Lowell on the road, remember? He mentioned us evacuees and Mrs Beesley said she hadn't seen us.'

Adam grunted. 'It's like she told you at the time,' he said. 'That old man's a busybody. If he knew you was at the 'ouse, he'd most likely tell everyone.'

Peter chewed on a chunk of bread. 'Well, what's wrong with that? Is it supposed to be a secret?'

'No, course not. It's just . . . people in these parts . . .'

'Like to keep themselves to themselves,' finished Peter. 'Well, he knows all about us now, doesn't he? He knows we're there.'

'Hmm.' Adam scowled. 'I don't know what they'll have to say about that.'

'They?'

'Mr Sheldon and Mrs B. They was quite particular that they didn't want him to know about you and Daisy.'

'But I don't understand, why would they care about that?'

'If you'd stop prattlin' on for a minute,' said Adam, 'I might be able to grab forty winks.' He took a last drag on his roll up and flicked the butt in the general direction of the lake.

'Sorry,' muttered Peter. 'I was only chatting.'

'Yeah, well don't,' Adam told him. 'Just let me get a bit of shut-eye.'

Peter wondered what was wrong with Adam. Why was he being so grumpy about everything? And what exactly was the secret he was trying to keep? Peter sat there, eating his lunch and watching Adam as he gradually succumbed to sleep. It took a little while, but eventually his eyes closed and his breathing became slow and rhythmic. Peter waited until he was sure that Adam wasn't going to wake up again. Then he reached carefully into his bag and took out the book the professor had given him. He studied it, keeping it behind the knapsack just in case Adam woke up. It was a slim volume backed with pale green boards. On the cover, in gold leaf, were the words, *Romney Marsh: A History* and underneath it, *Professor D. Lowell B.A., M.Sc., Ph.D.* Peter opened the book and scanned the contents page thoughtfully, looking for something that might catch his attention. He noticed one chapter heading that did exactly that.

CAPTAIN MICHEAUX AND THE MYSTERY OF
SHELDON GRANGE

Turning to the relevant page, Peter scanned the rows of tiny black print and paused when one line caught his attention. He began to read.

Captain Jean Micheaux was a fascinating character. Contemporary accounts describe him as a strict disciplinarian, a man twice decorated for bravery in the Napoleonic Wars. At the age of sixty-five, he could easily have progressed to a higher rank, but he'd always refused such offers. He wanted nothing more than to lead his men and felt that a captain was the rank for which he had been destined. He was also, interestingly, a skilled musician.

He was adept at playing the flageolet or French pipe, one that he'd made himself and which he claimed to have carved from the leg bone of one of his enemies! He carried it with him everywhere and was known for breaking into a jaunty tune at the drop of a tricorn hat.

Peter stopped reading for a moment. A flageolet. A pipe. Could that be the sound he'd heard echoing across the Marsh at night? He continued reading.

It's fascinating to imagine the scene. The prisoners of war, toiling away in the hot sun with their picks and shovels as they worked on the endless digging of the canal; and then, in the lunch break, when the men sat down to eat their meagre rations, the captain taking out his pipe and playing a favourite melody. Little wonder that Micheaux was so popular with the men he commanded.

One of the local landowners and the man who was chiefly responsible for employing the French prisoners in this area was one Jeremiah Sheldon…

Peter frowned. Sheldon? Did that mean the man was related to Mr Sheldon, who owned the Grange now? Reading on, Peter's suspicion was immediately confirmed.

Jeremiah, of course, was the man who built Sheldon Grange back in 1742, and the great-great-grandfather of the present occupier, Mr Alfred Sheldon.

There's no real proof, but the gossip at the time suggests that in order to get the French prisoners of war to work on the canal, Jeremiah may have made Captain Micheaux an offer, promising him that if he and his men would work on the canal without argument and without trying to escape, then he would see to it that when the task was completed, the prisoners would be granted their freedom. With the gift of hindsight, it's all too easy to see that Jeremiah probably never had such powers at his command. But Micheaux must have believed that he did, and as a consequence he committed his men to four and a half years of backbreaking toil.

Work on the canal was completed in September 1808. One can only imagine how the prisoners must have dreamed of finishing work and getting home to their families. Micheaux had even gone to the lengths of purchasing several identical dolls from a local trader, which he intended to take back for his daughters, of whom he was very proud. He had six of them, and the youngest, Josette, just eight years old, he had not seen since she was a baby. Micheaux must have fully believed that he would soon be free to return to France. But it was not to be.

We must now move into the area of supposition, but it's easy enough to imagine how events might have unfolded after this. Micheaux would doubtless have gone to Jeremiah, to demand that he fulfil his promise and release the prisoners. Clearly he was not happy with the answer he received. One local writer, Michael Williams, who kept a diary at the time, records having heard somebody he refers to only as 'The Frenchman', shouting and cursing and swearing revenge on those who had deceived him. The date was 5th September 1808, only a few days after work had finished on the canal. Micheaux (assuming it was him) was also heard threatening to write a letter to the authorities, telling how he and his men had been duped by their captors. I do not doubt that the captain's words would have carried considerable weight.

But, puzzlingly, those concerns were never aired. Williams' account is the last mention ever made of Captain Micheaux. After that, he and his troops simply disappeared from the records. From that date on, there's no mention of them in any documents... and believe me, I have looked.

It would be delightful, would it not, to imagine that Micheaux and his men were sent safely back to their mother country to be greeted by the outstretched arms of their loved ones? But I fear this was not the case. After much soul-searching, I have arrived at the inevitable conclusion that something happened to Micheaux and his men. Something unspeakable.

This suspicion was confirmed for me when I visited the crypt at St Leonard's Church in Hythe, a place where I know for a fact the prisoners of war were housed at one point. Any casual visitor to the crypt can hardly fail to notice a dated inscription chiselled into the wall in French, some kind of quotation, people have suggested, though I tend to think of it more as a curse...

The sudden loud bleating of a sheep made Peter look up. He glanced at Adam, anxious that the sound might have wakened him, but he was still fast asleep, his chest rising and falling with a steady rhythm. Peter returned his attention to the book, realising that he had lost his place. He scanned the page again until another sentence caught his eye.

What happened next has all the qualities of a Gothic horror story. For that, the author can only apologise, but the facts are as undeniable as they are inexplicable. I speak of course, of the series of disasters that have occurred at Sheldon Grange and the surrounding area over the passing centuries. I refer, more specifically, to the drownings.

The first incident occurred almost exactly one year after the completion of the canal. The initial death was that of Jeremiah Sheldon's eight-year-old daughter, Mary. The official police investigation claims that the girl went out alone, late at night on 7th September 1809. Nobody seems to have the slightest idea why she might have done such a thing. Her body was discovered floating in the canal the following day. She was barefoot and dressed in her nightgown.

Peter felt a sense of cold dread settling in his stomach. He was thinking of the children he and Daisy had seen dancing in the garden last night – the way Daisy had wanted to go out to join them. And he was thinking about the dream, the awful dream of a girl's face rising up out of the waters of the canal. He continued to read.

Had it been just the one death, the matter might have been dismissed as no more than an unhappy accident. But six years later, Jeremiah's brother, Michael, living barely half a mile from the Grange, lost his daughter, Hannah, in exactly the same manner. Chillingly, the date was 9th September – and Hannah, too, was eight years old.

It was to be by no means the last death. Twelve years later, Jeremiah's son, Thomas, lost his daughter, Sybil. How did she die? She drowned in Thursby Lake, out in the wilds of Romney Marsh. It happened on the 7th September 1827. Sybil was eight years old.

Peter paused. Thursby Lake? Hadn't Adam said that was the name of *this* lake? He glanced up from the book and stared at the muddy banks sloping down to the still olive-green water, but everything looked normal enough. He returned his attention to the book.

Three deaths by drowning. All of them in September. All eight-year-old girls from the Sheldon family. Surely too much to pass off as coincidence? People around Romney Marsh started talking of a curse.

There were no girls born into the Sheldon clan for a very long time. But tragedy still haunted the family. It would be a time-consuming task indeed to piece together the seemingly endless list of disasters that have befallen them over the years. Suffice to say that it comprises accidents, illnesses and untimely deaths. But death by drowning seems to have been exclusively reserved for the young girls of the family.

On 7th September 1874, a descendant of Jeremiah's, Oliver Sheldon, the latest owner of the Grange, lost his only child, an eight-year-old daughter, Alison. Again, she drowned in the canal in an almost identical scenario to her ancestors. Accounts of the time claim that she went out, barefoot, in the middle of the night. Some people suggested she might have been sleepwalking. It's interesting to note that she had two older brothers, but they were both unharmed. In every case, it was the daughter who died. If no female victims were available, it seemed, the curse moved on, leaving the male children unharmed. Once again, the more superstitious inhabitants of the Marsh began to talk in hushed whispers about the existence of something that came to be known as 'The Sheldon Curse'. And those who knew their history recalled that Captain Micheaux's youngest child, Josette, had been eight years old when the captain and his men finished work on the canal and... disappeared.

These beliefs were given more credence when it transpired that Alison was not to be the last fatality. Oliver's brother, William, lost his eight-year-old daughter, Anne, only four years later on 7th September. His other brother, Thomas lost his daughter, Sarah, six years after that on 9th September. She too, was in her eighth year. And how did the girls die? They drowned. Anne met her end, once again in the Military Canal. Thomas Sheldon was no longer living in the area. He'd moved to London, where perhaps he believed his children would be safe from the curse. But his daughter Sarah was found drowned in the boating lake at a local park. Nobody knew how she had come to be there.

Always an eight-year-old daughter. Always the Sheldon family. And, so it would seem, it didn't matter where the victims lived. All in all, it was a blessing that for a very long time, no more female children were born into the family.

Those who have investigated the curse have always

asked the same question. Why that date? Why 7th September or shortly thereafter? I would direct them to visit the church of St Leonard and to look at the inscription. Then it all makes perfect sense.

And one must arrive at the inevitable conclusion. If you are a member of the Sheldon family and you are a girl, then you are doomed to die in your eighth year… on or shortly after the 7th September. I can find no evidence of any Sheldon girl who has managed to outlive that fateful month.

Peter lifted his eyes from the book in sudden realisation. September. But… that was now! And… he felt the heat rising within him as he worked out the date. He and Daisy had left home on the first of September. They'd been here exactly a week. Which made today… the seventh of September. And Miss Sally was eight years old.

He felt suddenly chilled to the bone, as though the dull glare of the sun had lost all its power. He was sure now that the professor was no madman – and he understood exactly why Mrs Beesley and Adam had wanted to keep his and Daisy's presence at the Grange quiet. Daisy wasn't a Sheldon, but she was almost the same age and size as Sally.

Did Sheldon and Mrs Beesley think that they might be able to pass her off in place of Miss Sally?

A thin, bleating sound cut across his thoughts and he glanced up to the edge of the lake, where a sheep had wandered too close to the water and had bogged itself down in the soft mud. It was looking towards him, baaing helplessly.

Peter returned the book to his knapsack and prodded one of Adam's feet with his own. Adam grunted and stirred.

'Wassup?' he muttered.

'What's today's date?'

Adam glared up at him. 'How should I know?'

'It's the seventh, isn't it?'

'If you say so. Why did you wake me?'

'There's a sheep stuck in the mud.'

'Well, go and get 'im out then,' came the surly reply.

'But...'

'Go on, boy. Can't you see I'm restin'?'

Peter muttered something under his breath and got to his feet. He trudged towards the lake, but his mind was elsewhere. He was thinking about Daisy and telling himself that he needed to get to her, to make sure she was all right. He tried to assure himself that nothing could happen to her before nightfall, that the bad things didn't seem to happen until darkness had fallen; and besides, the curse wasn't meant for her but for Miss Sally. And yet...

He got to the sheep and grabbed a couple of handfuls of wool on its back, then began to tug at the creature, trying to pull it back from the water's edge, but the wool just came away in clumps. The sheep stood there, bleating stupidly for a moment, then managed to raise one foot with a squelching sound. Now Peter put his arms around the creature's neck and pulled harder, grunting with the effort. The sheep got another foot free and began to scramble away from the water, heading back towards her companions.

Peter straightened up. In the same instant, something moved in the water to his left, splashing the surface and Peter looked down, expecting to see the silvery flash of a fish in the shallows, but whatever was moving there was way too big to be a fish. Puzzled, he moved a step closer, placing his feet with care, mindful of getting himself bogged down like the sheep. He glanced back guiltily, but Adam was still stretched out on his coat, paying him no heed. Peter returned his gaze to the lake and a chill went through him as he registered something pale in the water, a white oval just below the surface, not in the shallows, but further off where the bottom dropped steeply away into darkness.

A face was staring blankly up at the sky, a girl's face, but horribly wasted and shrivelled, as though bleached by the water. There was an impression of strands of dark hair swaying around the head like an unspeakable halo. Peter's first thought was that he was looking at something dead, but then the head turned slightly to one side and the eyes gazed up at him, regarding him with a horrible intensity.

He saw all this for a fraction of a second, no more, and then there was another swirl and the face was gone, swallowed whole by those dark depths. That was when fear jolted in Peter's chest, snatching his breath away and pushing him back from the water's edge as surely as an out-thrust hand to his chest. He turned and hurried back to Adam, trying to control his breathing, telling himself that he was imagining things, he had to be, but knowing at the same time that he had seen *something* in the water, something that had no right to be there.

He reached Adam and stood over him, gazing down at him in disgust. Then he directed another fierce kick against the sleeping man's foot. Adam jolted awake with a curse and sat up, staring at Peter indignantly.

'What's got into you?' he cried.

'I'm going,' said Peter. 'I'm heading back to the Grange.'

'What do you mean? You can't just up and go when you *feel* like it.'

'Try and stop me,' cried Peter. He leaned over, grabbed his knapsack and swung it across his shoulder. Then he began to stride back in the direction from which he thought he'd come, but everywhere looked exactly the same, endless stretches of flat green marsh dotted with hundreds of white, woolly shapes. He kept going though, telling himself that he would find his way somehow.

After a few moments, he heard Adam's footsteps thudding on the ground behind him. 'Hey, 'old on a minute. What's the big hurry?'

Peter gritted his teeth, but slowed his pace a little to allow Adam to catch up with him. The old man was gasping for breath when he fell in beside Peter. He'd pulled on his coat and picked up his own knapsack before following.

'You can't just go... charging off like that,' he protested. 'You ain't even... goin' the right way. A greenhorn like you, you could wander into a bog and drown yourself. What would I tell Mr Sheldon then?'

Peter sneered. 'I'd say that would be very handy for you all,' he muttered. 'Then I'd be out of the way and you'd have Daisy all to yourselves.'

Adam gave a derisive laugh. 'What are you talkin' about? I reckon you've been out in the sun too long. You're beginning to ramble.'

'Are you going to show me the way back or not?' snapped Peter.

'Just 'old yer 'orses a minute. I'll get you back, but we've a job to do first. You...you want to send that postcard, don't you? You've been nagging Mrs B about it for days. We can head back through Hythe and drop the card off on the way. If we don't take it now, Lord knows when we'll get another chance. You...need to let your parents know that everything is all right, don't you?'

Peter narrowed his eyes. He wanted to send the postcard, of course he did, but he couldn't help feeling that the cheery little note he and Daisy had put together for Mum would be nothing short of a lie.

Beside the return address, they had written:

Dear Mum,
How are you? We're keeping well. Romney Marsh is very big and green. Have you heard anything from Dad? We are looking forward

175

to this war being over, so we can come home to you.

Love from Daisy and Peter

'I do want to send it,' he said. 'Mum must be going mad with worry. But...it's *not* all right here, is it? There's something going on. Something you don't want to tell me about.'

'I...I can't, lad. I don't even know what I think myself any more!'

'*I* know I just saw something in the lake over there.'

'Something in the lake?' Adam looked puzzled. 'Like what?'

'A face. Looking at me.' Peter realised how ridiculous that sounded, but no words could have conveyed the horror of what had stared at him from the shallows. 'Some kind of ghost,' he added. 'Somebody drowned.' He thought for a moment about what he'd read in the professor's book. 'Sybil,' he said, remembering. 'Sibyl Sheldon.'

'In daylight?' Adam looked worried. 'You don't normally see things in the daytime. I've only ever seen them after dark.'

'So you admit there is something?'

Adam shrugged his shoulders and sighed. 'Oh aye, what's the use in pretending? The Marsh is haunted all right. Always has been. There's stories about this area would turn

176

your hair white. And I've seen things out here at night.' His eyes got big and round as though he could see them now. 'Things I couldn't explain. Things that scared me near witless. That's why none of us wants to be out after dark. But…ghosts is one thing. All that stuff about the Sheldon Curse…that's just nonsense, that is, made up by people with too much time on their 'ands.'

'But what about the music?'

Adam shrugged. 'I ain't never 'eard no music,' he said. 'Miss Sally hears it all right and I know you and Daisy heard it that first time we was out here. And I'm not saying that any of you are crazy, but…ghosts is ghosts, Peter. They're just…bad memories. It's not as if they can 'urt anybody.'

'You really believe that? After everything that's happened? All those deaths in the Sheldon Family?'

'Oh, that's just coincidence! I tried telling Mrs B that, but she wouldn't have it. She said the bad times was coming back.' He shook his head. 'She and Mr Sheldon, they've been thinking like this ever since his wife died. But it was just a terrible accident, nothing more. Sheer bad luck. I told 'em, there's no curse, that's all stuff and nonsense. But would they listen to me?'

'I think there *is* a curse,' said Peter grimly. 'Tonight is the seventh of September and Miss Sally is eight years old, so...'

Adam groaned. 'It's that damned professor, isn't it? He's got you believing his nonsense.'

'It's not nonsense, Adam. It's all there in his book. The dates, the names, everything.'

'His book? When did you read that?'

'Never mind. It's all there in black and white. I think Mrs Beesley is planning something and...well, it looks like you're helping her.'

Adam shook his head. 'You've got to understand something, Peter. It's not me, it's *them*. I have to do what they tell me. Mrs B said if I didn't play along, they'd turf me out. I'm an old man, that stable is all I've got in the world. What would I do if they fired me?'

Peter looked at him and tried to be sympathetic. 'They don't own you,' he said. 'They can't make you do things you don't want to do.'

'I wouldn't be so sure.' Adam gave a long sigh. 'Look,' he said. 'It's true Mrs B wanted you out of the way today...but not for the reasons you think.'

'Oh no?'

'No! She told me she just wanted them two girls to have a bit of time on their own, so they could really make friends.'

'You believe that?' said Peter. 'Oh, come on, Adam. And it just so happens she wants me out of the way tonight – the seventh of September?'

Adam laughed. 'That don't mean nothin'. No harm is going to come to Miss Sally, not when they keep her in that room, night and day. You'll see, tonight will come and go and they'll see what nonsense it was. And won't they feel like a pair of chumps then?'

'It's not Miss Sally I'm worried about,' said Peter. 'It's Daisy. I . . . keep thinking something bad is going to happen to her.'

'But 'ow could it? Even if you believed any of that nonsense, she isn't even a Sheldon, is she? So how could *she* be in any danger?'

'It's just this feeling I have . . . that they're planning to hurt her in some way.'

Adam considered this for a moment.

'Look, come with me to Hythe,' he said. 'We'll post that card to your mother. We'll head back to the Grange from there. How does that suit you?'

'If you're playing for time,' Peter warned him. 'I'll . . .'

'Don't be daft. I told you I'll get you back, and I will. You needn't worry on that score.'

Peter scowled. 'You promise?'

Adam looked shifty. 'I'll get you back,' he repeated.

'By nightfall?' added Peter.

'Yes, yes, whatever you want.' He looked nervously around. 'I've no great wish to be out here after dark, anyway,' he said.

'I thought you said ghosts couldn't hurt you?'

'No, but they can still scare me.'

'All right then,' said Peter. 'We'll go to Hythe. Just long enough to post that card.' He looked around. 'I suppose you'd better lead the way.'

Adam angled sharply to his left and moved through the herd of sheep, making them scatter before him. Peter had no option but to follow. He glanced at the sky and saw that the sun was already beginning its slow journey down towards the western horizon. He tried not to think about what he had just seen in the green waters of the lake, rising up like a premonition. He wondered if this place was turning him mad, making him see things that weren't really there. He almost wished that were the case. Part of him just wanted to run, run in whichever direction he thought might take him back to his sister, but he made himself place one foot in front of the other as he and Adam made their way across the seemingly endless stretches of the Marsh.

CHAPTER EIGHTEEN

Hythe turned out to be a pretty little town, but Peter was in no mood to appreciate its picturesque charms. Adam led the way along narrow winding streets, cutting back and forth between ranks of white-painted cottages, clearly knowing exactly where he was headed. They called first at the small post office, where Peter handed the stamped postcard across to a stern-looking woman behind the counter, who assured him it would go in the first post the following morning. He and Adam emerged into the afternoon sunlight and started a slow climb uphill. Peter clumped glumly along behind Adam, his apprehension mounting by the minute. As the time passed, he was growing more and more agitated.

'Why are we still here?' he asked. 'We've posted the card.'

Adam looked as though he was regretting ever having taken Peter out.

'I've just got a quick errand to run before we head back. I won't be long.'

'Please hurry. I'm worried about Daisy.'

Adam snorted. 'She'll be fine. I told you, she's in no danger.'

They turned a corner and found themselves outside a tumbledown old building with black and white timbered walls. A sign hanging above the door announced that this was the *Smuggler's Retreat*. The sign featured a painting of an old sailing ship that had foundered on rocks. In the foreground, a shifty-looking man with an eye patch and a tricorn hat held a lantern. Adam nodded towards the closed wooden door.

'I got to pop in 'ere for a bit,' he said. 'You wait, I won't be long.'

'It's a *pub*,' said Peter suspiciously.

'You don't say?' Adam gave him a wide-eyed look. 'I need to talk to the landlord, that's all.'

'What about?'

'Never you mind, "what about"! I got a bit of business with 'im, ain't I? Now I already told you, I won't be long. You just wait 'ere for me.'

'Can't I come in?' asked Peter.

'No,' said Adam firmly. 'Youngsters ain't allowed in there. You just cool yer 'eels for a bit.'

'And then we'll head straight back to the Grange?'

'Yes, yes, just as you say! Lord, you're worse than Mrs B, you are.' Adam went to the door of the pub and pushed it open. Peter glimpsed a press of shadowy figures inside and the smell of stale beer belched out onto the street, making him wrinkle his nose. Adam stepped inside and the door slammed shut again.

Peter stood there for a few moments, staring at it blankly, wondering what he was supposed to do now. He turned and looked around, searching for something to occupy him. The street was deserted. Up at the top of the hill, he could see the entrance to a church. It looked like a church from a storybook, he thought, a big old building of grey stone with a square tower at one end and turrets sticking up from each corner. In front of it there was a wooden sign and printed on it in ornate golden letters were the words PARISH CHURCH OF ST LEONARD.

This immediately rang a bell in Peter's head. He'd seen that name recently but for a moment he couldn't think where. Then it came to him. He reached into his knapsack and took out Professor Lowell's book. He found the chapter he'd been reading earlier. Searching through it, he soon found what he was looking for.

> *...the crypt at St Leonard's Church in Hythe, a place where I know for a fact the prisoners of war were billeted at one point. Any casual visitor to the crypt can hardly fail to notice a dated inscription chiselled into the wall in French, some kind of quotation, people have suggested, though I tend to think of it more as a curse. The infamous Sheldon Curse, perhaps?*

Peter read the next paragraph, something he had missed before.

> *I urge readers to visit the church themselves and take a cold hard look at the contents of the crypt. And pay particular attention to the date beside the inscription, something that I believe was inscribed on the captain's final night on this earth. I'm absolutely sure that you will reach the same inevitable and chilling conclusion as me.*

Peter frowned, slipped the book back into his knapsack, glanced at the closed door of the pub and decided that it could be some time before Adam emerged from there. So he started walking further up the hill. He hesitated for only a moment at the heavy wooden doors of the church, gazing back down the street to reassure himself that there was still no sign of Adam. Then he went inside.

He found himself standing in the dark, echoey interior, looking straight ahead to the nave, which was dominated by three huge stained-glass windows and a high, vaulted ceiling. He gazed around, wondering which way to go.

'Can I help you?' A vicar had come out of a doorway to his right, a plump, middle-aged fellow dressed in a tweed jacket with the white dog collar showing at the top of his black shirt. He had neatly brushed grey hair and blue eyes that twinkled behind wire-framed spectacles.

'I was...looking for something,' said Peter awkwardly. 'Something I...er...read about.'

The vicar's smile faded a little. 'I think I can guess what that would be,' he said. 'It's why a lot of people visit the church these days. Sadly, not enough of them seem to be coming in order to pray.' He smiled to show that he was only joking. 'I'm the Reverend Latimer, the parish priest here at

St Leonard's. May I enquire where you read about this … something?'

'In a book,' said Peter. 'A … history book.'

Reverend Latimer sighed. 'This wouldn't, by any chance, be Professor Lowell's book, would it?'

Peter nodded. 'Do you know him?'

'Oh yes, I know him,' said Reverend Latimer, but he didn't sound particularly pleased about it. 'When the professor approached me to say that he was writing a history of the Marsh and that he wanted to include a chapter about the church, I was of course delighted. And I did everything I could to help him with his research.' He scowled. 'Then the book was published and I read it.' He made a face as though he suddenly had a bad taste in his mouth. 'A lot of people around here read it. It got this sleepy little community into a fair old tizzy, I'm afraid. I must say, I'm surprised that a young lad like you should have seen it.'

'The professor gave me a copy,' said Peter.

'Did he now?' Reverend Latimer looked as though he disapproved. 'Now, why doesn't that surprise me? I think the good professor is a bit of a self-publicist in his spare time. He … didn't take money off you, did he?'

'No. He wanted to warn me. You see, I'm . . . I'm staying at Sheldon Grange.'

'Ah.' The reverend looked perturbed by this news. 'Well, I'm not going to say that I believe any of the fanciful claims the professor makes in his so-called history, but . . . I can see how it might trouble somebody who happens to be staying there. You're a relative of the Sheldons, I suppose?'

'No, sir. I'm an evacuee. From London.'

'Hmm. Of course, I did hear that several of you had been sent out here. It was all organised by the Quakers, wasn't it?'

'Yes, sir.'

'Must be difficult for you, leaving home and all that. You can only have been here a short time?'

'A week.'

'And I expect you're missing your family terribly.'

Peter nodded. 'Yes, sir. It's not just me. There's my little sister, Daisy. It's her I'm most worried about.'

The reverend nodded. He seemed to think for a few moments before he replied. 'I can appreciate that the stories you've heard about the Grange's history may have unsettled you. But . . . I'm sorry, what was your name . . . ?'

'Peter, sir.'

'Well, Peter, at times of duress, it's easy, isn't it, to let your imagination run away with you? The point I wish to make is that things that seem strange and forbidding to us when we glimpse them in the dark can easily be explained in the cold light of day.'

Peter didn't have anything to say to this. He was thinking of something that he couldn't explain, that bleached white face staring up at him from the cold depths of the lake only an hour or so earlier – and in broad daylight. He considered mentioning the incident to the priest, but knew instantly that he would be disbelieved. So he tried something less likely to be challenged.

'We hear music, sir. At night.'

'Music?' The reverend raised his eyebrows. 'Well, our Mr Simmons does practise on the organ late some nights and people have occasionally complained about the volume. It's amazing how sound can carry across these flat lands.'

Peter shook his head. 'It's a flute, sir. Or a...fladgy...' He didn't quite know how to say the word. 'A French pipe.'

The reverend studied Peter for a moment. 'A term that I believe is mentioned in the professor's book. Do you not think, Peter, that his account has set your mind working in a certain direction, and that—'

'It can't be that, sir,' interrupted Peter. 'You see, I only read the book this afternoon, but I've heard the music several times over the week. And I saw…'

'You saw what?'

It was in Peter's mind to describe what he'd witnessed the previous night, the pale-faced girls, lurching and swaying around the garden in time to that unearthly music, but somehow he couldn't bring himself to put that into words either. It had also occurred to him that Adam might very well have emerged from the pub by now and be marching around outside, looking for Peter and cursing his bad luck for having the thankless task of minding the boy for a day. So he simply looked enquiringly around the nave and said, 'The crypt?'

The reverend looked uneasy at this but he bowed his head and turned away. 'Follow me,' he said. 'I'm far from happy about your reasons for wanting to see it, but it's open to public view, so who am I to talk you out of it?' He glanced over his shoulder as he walked. 'We call it the crypt but that's not strictly accurate. It should really be called a charnel house or an ossuary.'

They came to a small arched doorway in one wall and sure enough, beside it there was a little wooden sign that read, *To the crypt*. The priest reached out and flicked a switch on the wall.

'You have electricity,' observed Peter, and then thought how stupid that sounded. 'They still use paraffin lamps at the Grange. And battery wireless.'

The reverend nodded. 'I dare say it'll be some time before they manage to run cables out to that wilderness,' he said. 'We've only just had this system installed. It's helped enormously. With the old gas lamps we had, some visitors tended to let their imaginations get the better of them.' He swung open the wooden door, revealing a set of stone steps leading down. 'Now, follow me and please don't be nervous.'

This last remark puzzled Peter, but he said nothing. He followed Reverend Latimer through the doorway and down the steps. It was only a short distance but it was like stepping into another world. They reached level ground and went through a second doorway and into a long, gloomily lit corridor with a doorway at each end. At first, Peter wasn't quite sure what he was looking at. He was aware of what appeared to be a long, spiky off-white hedge, running along one side of the wall ahead of him. Then his gaze focused and he couldn't stop himself from drawing in his breath.

Bones. He was looking at bones. Not just a few, but hundreds, probably thousands of them. They were piled to head height all along the left-hand side of the corridor ahead of him, with a narrow channel between it and the right-hand wall. They were mostly arm or leg bones, Peter guessed, but with several skulls piled decoratively on top. A sign warned people not to touch them, though Peter couldn't imagine that anyone would actually *want* to.

'Are they real?' he heard himself asking, and his own voice sounded strange to his ears, halting and full of dread.

'Oh yes,' said the reverend, leading the way along the narrow corridor. 'Young people like yourself seem to be fond of figures, so I'll just tell you that there are eight thousand thigh bones down here and over two thousand skulls.' He reached the end of the bone wall and led Peter around a corner. At the end of a shorter stretch of corridor, there were two huge arch-shaped alcoves set into the walls, on either side of a third arch, the upper half of which was a latticed window, through which a harsh light spilled. Each alcove had rows of wooden shelves running across it and each shelf was neatly stacked with human skulls, their blank eye sockets staring sightlessly out at the two people standing in front of them.

'Golly,' said Peter. He couldn't think of anything else to say right now.

There was a long, deep silence then, as he and the reverend stood there, looking up at the serried ranks of death. Finally, Peter had to ask a question: 'Who were they?'

Reverend Latimer frowned. 'Nobody's really sure,' he admitted. 'Oh, there are all kinds of theories. Some say that they're the remains of foreign soldiers who died in a great battle. Others think they might be victims of the Black Death, though that's unlikely because most remains were buried in quicklime to prevent the plague from spreading.' He gazed up at the skulls as though seeking inspiration. 'The likeliest explanation is that they're just the bones of local people, dug up from the graveyard when the church was extended in the thirteenth century. The local authorities wanted to keep them on consecrated ground, but had to make room in the graveyard for new bodies. So they raised the floor of the chancel and had this corridor built beneath it to house the bones. Over the years, I suppose the collection has been ... added to.'

'You mean that ... if you die around here, they stick your bones in this place?' cried Peter.

The reverend stared at him for a moment and then smiled.

'Oh, not any more,' he insisted. 'No, these date back a long way. Some people think they may even go back to Roman times.'

Gazing up at the skulls, something else occurred to Peter, something that Professor Lowell had hinted at in the book, but hadn't actually said.

I'm absolutely sure that like me, you will reach the same inevitable and chilling conclusion.

The thought struck him like an open hand across the face.

'They're *here*, aren't they?' he gasped. 'The French prisoners of war? Their bones could be hidden anywhere amongst this lot.'

The reverend snorted. 'It's a theory,' he admitted. 'Some would say a crackpot theory. And it's certainly what Professor Lowell was hinting at in that book of his. Of course, it's all speculation. And there'd be no way of finding out whether there's any truth in it.'

'So . . . you don't think it's true?'

The reverend sighed. 'Somebody who believes in a thing can write about it in a way that makes it all seem very feasible,' he admitted. 'But it doesn't necessarily make it the truth.'

'That's pretty much what Adam said.'

'Adam?'

'Oh, just somebody who works at the Grange.' The mention of Adam brought Peter's mind back to his reason for coming in here. 'What about the inscription?' he asked. 'The one the professor mentions.'

Reverend Latimer frowned. 'Oh *that*,' he said. 'Here.' He led Peter closer to the wall between the alcoves and pointed out some words that were cut into the stone, just under the window.

Peter reached out a hand and traced them with his fingertips, noting how exquisitely carved they were, the letters deeply incised, ornate and graceful. It must have taken ages to chisel them into the hard stone. But he could see at a glance that it wasn't written in English.

Qui paie les pipeaux commande la musique.
J.M. 7 Septembre 1808

'It's really here,' he murmured.

'Oh yes,' agreed the reverend. 'A genuine piece of historic graffiti, that. Professor Lowell noticed it when he first visited the crypt. I didn't realise that he would attach quite so much importance to it . . . or that he would suggest that this 'J. M.' could be the Micheaux character.'

'Well, it all seems to fit,' said Peter. 'The date's right, the initials are the same . . . and it's in French, isn't it?'

'Yes. But that's really no great surprise. There were quite a few French prisoners of war housed in this area around that time. And the church records do mention that some of them were imprisoned down here for a couple of nights when the regular jail became flooded. But that isn't proof, Peter. Who's to say that it's not somebody else with those initials?'

Peter looked at Reverend Latimer. 'It sounds to me as though you don't *want* to believe it,' he said.

The reverend looked uncomfortable. 'A lot of people got very upset by the professor's theories,' he said. 'You must remember, many of the families he mentioned still have descendants living around here. I'm sure no reputable publisher would have agreed to put out the book, but as I understand it he paid for the publishing himself. What they call a vanity project. Thankfully, it doesn't seem to have sold in great numbers anywhere beyond the Marsh.' He glared at Peter. 'Can you imagine how it would feel? Somebody suggesting that your ancestors took part in a . . . murder? Little wonder the professor is now about as popular as the bubonic plague.' He shook his head. 'He's had threats, you know. The windows of his house smashed, warnings to leave if he knows what's good for him. His housekeeper walked out and I know he's been unable to get a replacement. And some people have been less than charitable towards me. They've said that if I hadn't helped him with his research in the first place, the book would never have seen the light of day. But how could I have known what he was going to write?'

Peter returned his attention to the words on the wall. 'What does it say?' he asked.

The reverend looked at the words again, as though he'd forgotten they were there. 'It's a familiar enough phrase in English: Who pays the piper, calls the tune.'

'What does that even mean?'

The reverend considered for a moment. 'Well, basically, it means ... whoever pays the musician gets to choose the songs that are played. And I suppose, if you haven't paid then you don't have any right to complain if you don't like what you hear.'

Peter thought about that. About the music he'd heard in the night. What would you call a man who plays the French pipe? Why, a piper, of course.

'Micheaux wasn't paid,' he murmured.

'I beg your pardon?'

'Captain Micheaux. He was supposed to be paid for all the work he and his men did on the canal, by being allowed to go home to his family in France.'

'Yes, but, Peter…'

'But Jeremiah Sheldon refused to pay him what he'd promised. So Sheldon got the music for free, didn't he? Maybe…maybe Micheaux decided to play a different tune, one that came with its own price. Sheldon had to pay for the music with the…the life of a daughter…'

'Now you see, this is exactly why I was reluctant to bring you down here in the first place. That's nothing but fanciful nonsense!'

Peter pointed to the date. 'Seventh of September,' he said. And another realisation hit him. 'The professor thinks he probably carved this on the night he died. That's why he always comes back on that date. To claim his fee.' He looked at Reverend Latimer. 'All the girls died on or after the seventh. I think the music starts before then, but the seventh is when it's at its strongest. The first time I heard it, it was faint, but it seems to get louder every time I hear it. I suppose some of the girls were able to hang on a bit longer, but the music kept calling to them and, in the end, they had to go out and face it.' He took a breath. 'Tonight is the seventh,' he said, 'Tonight, Micheaux will come looking for an eight-year-old girl...'

An image flashed into Peter's mind. A picture of Daisy, her expression one of terror, her hands held up in a vain attempt to ward off an attack. He felt as though somebody had pumped his veins full of cold water.

'I have to go,' he said.

'Peter, are you all right? You've gone quite pale.'

Peter ignored the reverend. He turned and walked away from him, heading back round the corner and moving past the head-high stack of bones. His heart was beating like a sledgehammer in his chest and his mouth was dry. Reverend Latimer came after him, trying to get him to stop.

'Peter, hold on a moment. Let's talk. Let me at least get you a drink of tea or something...'

But then Peter was pounding up the short flight of steps and he was running across the nave, back towards the entrance doors.

'Peter!' The reverend's voice echoed around the church as Peter burst out from the doorway and ran back along the path to the street. He went straight downhill. When he got to the *Smuggler's Retreat*, there was still no sign of Adam, so he threw open the door and went inside. It was packed in there and heady with the smells of alcohol and pipe smoke. Adam was sitting on a stool at the bar, chatting happily with a red-faced man on the other side of the counter. Peter ran straight at Adam, grabbed his arm and nearly pulled him off the stool. Adam lurched round, his mouth open, the smell of whisky coming off him.

'What's up with you?' he shouted. 'Can't a fellow 'ave a quiet drink without somebody...'

But Peter was already pulling him towards the door.

'We're going back,' he snarled, his eyes burning into Adam's. 'We're going back right now, or I'm going without you.'

'Bless me, what's got into you, boy? 'Ave you gone stark raving mad?'

Maybe I have, thought Peter. Maybe that was exactly what had happened to him. Maybe he'd imagined everything he'd seen and heard since he arrived here and maybe Reverend Latimer was right about the professor's book. He didn't care about any of that. He only knew that he wasn't going to leave Daisy alone for a minute longer than he needed to. He managed to get Adam to the doorway.

People in the bar were calling out good-natured taunts.

'Where you off to, Adam? Mrs B needs you, does she?'

'Is that your new foreman? He looks young to be givin' the orders!'

'Hey, it was your round!'

'Sorry,' Adam shouted back. 'Gotta get back,' he grunted.

'But I thought you said you and the lad was staying 'ere tonight?' said the man behind the counter.

'Change of plan,' muttered Adam, and he glanced guiltily at Peter, as though he regretted him hearing that.

Then they were walking back along the narrow streets, Adam weaving unsteadily as he went, grumbling about how they were going home much earlier than they needed to, how they'd both be better off leaving the owners of the Grange to their own fanciful notions and getting away for one night. But Peter was horribly aware of how low the sun already was above the rooftops and he had no idea how long it would take them to get back to the Grange.

He had the distinct impression that something bad was coming, something that he couldn't see or hear or smell yet, but it was there all the same, just over the horizon, a heavy brooding malevolence that seemed to come closer with each passing moment. He was sure now that Daisy was in terrible danger and he prayed they'd be back at the Grange before it got dark.

CHAPTER NINETEEN

Peter and Adam strode across the Marsh, following the winding tracks that led through the riddle of bogs and lakes and waterways. Adam had clearly drunk quite a lot of whisky while Peter was in the church. His face was flushed red, his gait unsteady. Once or twice he even stumbled and had to throw out a hand to Peter's shoulder to steady himself.

It was getting late, the sun perilously close to the horizon. Peter kept thinking about how it had been the evening they'd arrived, the evident terror that Adam and Mrs Beesley had shown as darkness crept over the Marsh. He had no wish to repeat that experience. Especially since Adam had told him about the other ghosts out here.

'How much farther?' he asked anxiously.

'Not too far,' muttered Adam. 'Though I don't know what she'll have to say about it when we turn up out of the blue.'

'*She*? You mean, Mrs Beesley?'

Adam grunted. 'She'll be mad with me.' His former bravado seemed to be evaporating as they got closer to home. He was looking fearfully around, as though expecting to see something approaching. 'We shouldn't have come back so late.'

'I heard what that man said back at the pub,' Peter told him. 'He thought we were staying the night.'

'Did he say that?' Adam made a pathetic attempt at looking puzzled. 'He...probably thought it was too risky coming back in the twilight.'

'I thought you said ghosts can't hurt you?' said Peter.

'I don't mean that. It's just that it can be treacherous out here.'

'But you're supposed to know your way better than anyone, aren't you?

Adam could only shrug his shoulders. 'I'm just saying... in the dark and all that...it can be tricky.' He shook his head. 'I didn't want to be puttin' you in 'arm's way, that's all. I didn't think that one more night was going to make any difference.'

'So we *were* going to stay at the pub?'

'They're very nice rooms,' said Adam defensively. 'Like a

proper 'otel. Mrs B said she'd take care of the bill. I fancied a spot of luxury for one night. Sleeping in a soft, clean bed with proper pillows. Just for the novelty of it.'

'You said you'd get me back tonight. You *promised*.'

'To be fair, I never actually promised nothing.'

'You said we'd be back by nightfall.'

'I meant nightfall *tomorrow*! Look, you've got yourself all worked up over nothing. You surely don't think for one minute that your sister is in any kind of danger, do you? Mrs B might be an old nag, but she wouldn't harm anyone, especially a little girl.'

'I wish I had your faith in her. Don't you know what's been going on around here over the years? The drownings.'

'Yeah, I know about all that and I'll tell you what, I'm fed up with hearing about it. It's all anyone's ever talked about since that book came out a year ago. I told Mrs B, "It's just a load of made-up twaddle!"'

'But it's not twaddle,' insisted Peter. 'The things the professor said about Micheaux and the prisoners of war. It really happened, didn't it?'

'How would I know?' protested Adam. 'That was hundreds of years ago. Nobody knows what 'appened, people are just...guessin'.'

Peter looked at him. 'While you were drinking, I went into St Leonard's Church. I saw what was down in the crypt. Have you ever been there?'

Adam shook his head. 'Never 'ad much time for religion,' he admitted.

'That's not what I mean. The professor knew what he was talking about. Something bad did happen down there.'

'Who can say? There was a war on. The war against Napoleon. Bad things 'appen in a war, everyone knows that. And...there's some things that should be let lie. But busybodies like the professor, they goes poking their noses into the past and they opens up a whole bloomin' hornets' nest.'

'So you don't believe any of it? You don't believe that the music we hear at night is him – Micheaux?'

'Oh, for goodness sake...'

'Is that why you came to the Friends' Meeting House looking for children in the first place? So you could pay the Piper?'

Adam laughed but it sounded a little hysterical. 'The Piper! That's just a...bloomin' fairy tale.'

'So why were you there?'

'Mr Sheldon sent us. He said he wanted a companion for

Miss Sally, somebody to keep her company, what with her being so ill and everything. What's so bad about that?'

'But you got me as well. And that made things awkward, didn't it?'

'No, I...I was glad to see you. It was Mrs B who wasn't so happy about it. I don't know why. That woman... sometimes I think she's not the full shilling, if you know what I mean.' He shook his head. 'But I have to go along with her,' said Adam. 'I told you, she rules that house with an iron rod. And she'd throw me out without a moment's hesitation.'

'You don't even *live* in the house,' said Peter.

'The stable then! I'm an old man, Peter. I ain't got no family. Where would I go? How would I make a living?'

Peter didn't have an answer for that. 'Daisy had better be all right,' he said.

'Course she'll be all right,' Adam assured him. 'Why wouldn't she be? Look, whatever Mrs B and Mr Sheldon think is going to happen, and whatever you think you've found out, it's all nonsense. Imaginings. People putting two and two together and making five. I said it before and I'll say it again. Ghosts can't hurt you. They're just... puffs of smoke... bumps in the night. They aren't anything real.'

'But they *are*,' Peter said. 'I'm sure of it.'

Adam shook his head. He pointed, evidently relieved for a chance to change the subject. Off on the horizon there was the dark smudge of a building. The Grange.

Peter quickened his pace. 'Come on,' he said.

But Adam didn't hurry himself. He hung back allowing Peter to move further and further ahead of him. 'I'll go straight to the stables,' he called out. 'I wants to check on Bessie.'

Peter ignored him. He walked faster and faster and then, as he drew close to the house, broke into an impatient run. He raced in through the gates and up the track to the front door. He paused for a moment in the yard and turned to look back. The western sky was reddening as the sun began to slip out of sight and he had the distinct impression that out there something was gathering its strength, flexing its muscles, readying itself to return. He opened the door and stepped inside.

He strode along the hall, moving past the doorway of the sitting room. Mr Sheldon was slumped in his usual seat by the fire, but he lifted his head to look at Peter and his expression changed momentarily to one of dismay. He opened his mouth as if to say something, but nothing came out. The two of them stared at each other in silence for a moment. Peter became aware of the sound of a clock ticking. Then he began to feel uncomfortable, so he turned away. He continued along the hall and pushed open the kitchen door. Mrs Beesley was standing at the worktop, slicing a joint of meat with a huge knife. She turned in surprise at the sound of the door and, when she saw Peter, the knife slipped from her hand and clattered onto the tiled floor.

'What you doing back 'ere?' she asked him. It sounded like an accusation.

Peter stared defiantly back at her. 'Weren't you expecting me?' he asked, making no attempt to hide the sarcasm in his voice.

'I...I thought Adam was going to stay overnight in Hythe. I thought it would be...nice for you to see what the town was like.'

'The town?' Peter sneered. 'Or do you mean, the pub?'

'Where *is* Adam?' she asked, her voice steely.

'He's gone straight to the stables,' said Peter. 'Didn't seem keen on showing his face in here. Hiding from you, I expect.'

Mrs Beesley turned away and he got the distinct impression that she couldn't bring herself look him in the eye. She stooped, picked up the knife, wiped the blade on her apron, then went on with slicing the meat. 'Well then, since you're back, I...suppose I should do a little extra for supper,' she said. She was trying to sound as though everything was normal but failing badly. 'I imagine you're 'ungry?'

Peter continued to stare at the back of her head. He wasn't going to give her the satisfaction of an answer. 'Where's Daisy?' he asked.

'She's upstairs.'

'With Sally?'

'No, Miss Sally needed a bit of a rest. Daisy's in her room.'

'I'll go up and see her, then.'

'Suit yourself. I'll give you a call when supper's ready.'

Peter went back out into the hallway and headed for the staircase. He went up to the first floor. Miss Sally's door was shut and he could hear the muted sounds of a wireless playing within. He moved on to Daisy's room and began to open the door. He hesitated when he heard her voice. She seemed to be chatting happily to somebody.

'... then on my birthday, my mummy bought me some red velvet ribbons for my hair.'

A short pause.

'Yes, they were. Red's my favourite colour.'

Another pause.

'Oh, I don't know. I think that's a strange colour to like. I...'

Pause.

'Well, you would say that, wouldn't you!'

Peter pushed open the door as quietly as possible. Daisy was sitting on the far side of the four-poster bed. She was facing away from him, looking towards the window, where a row of dolls gazed blankly back at her. Daisy carried on talking.

'Yes, I'm looking forward to it!'

Pause.

'Of course I know how to dance!'

'Daisy?'

Peter took a step into the room and Daisy looked back over her shoulder in surprise. She smiled delightedly. 'Peter! You're back. They said you'd gone for the night. They said I wouldn't see you till tomorrow.'

'I bet they did.' Peter closed the door gently behind him, then walked around the bed and sat down beside her. 'Who...who were you talking to?' he asked her.

'Oh, just Tillie.'

'Daisy, listen to me. Tillie is a doll.'

'Shush!' Daisy looked very serious. 'She doesn't like it when you call her that. *She* thinks she's a little girl.'

Peter began to smile, but then the smile faded abruptly when he realised that she wasn't fooling around. Her expression was deadly serious. And then it came to him, something else he'd read in the professor's book.

Captain Micheaux had bought dolls from a local trader. Dolls he'd intended to take back to France. *Gifts for his daughters.* It was easy to imagine how his murderers might have taken the dolls as souvenirs and given them to their own children. Dolls that would become family heirlooms, handed down from generation to generation. One of them could certainly have ended up here at Sheldon Grange. Had the captain's spirit somehow found its way into those dolls?

He felt a cold ripple of fear trickling down his spine, making the short hairs on his back of his neck stand up.

'Daisy. I asked you this before,' he said. 'How…how do you know she's called…Tillie?'

'She told me. She says that's the name Miss Alison gave her.'

'Miss…Alison?' Peter thought he also remembered that name from Professor Lowell's book. Instinctively, he reached into his knapsack and took it out. He began to flick through the pages, looking for the right chapter.

'What's that?' asked Daisy.

'A book.'

'I can see that, silly, but what book?'

'It's a history of the Marsh, written by a local professor.'

'How did you get it?'

'He gave it to me. Professor Lowell, his name is. See, his name's on the cover. I met him when I was out on the Marsh with Adam and he told me to read it . . .'

'You met a *writer*?' Daisy looked astonished. 'Tillie, Peter says he met a writer. Imagine that!'

Peter glanced up for a moment and looked at the doll, dreading that he might see some kind of animation in that white china face. But she sat there with her companions, staring back at him, her eyes impossibly green, her tiny white teeth set in a mocking grin.

'Yes,' said Daisy. 'I think it's jolly exciting too!'

'Daisy, please stop talking for a moment. I'm trying to read.'

Then Peter found the bit he was looking for.

. . . on 7th September 1874, a descendant of Jeremiah's, Oliver Sheldon, the latest owner of the Grange, lost his only child, an eight-year-old daughter, Alison. Again, she drowned in the canal in an almost identical

scenario to her ancestors. Accounts of the time claim
that she went out, barefoot, in the middle of the night.
Some people suggested she might have been
sleepwalking...

Dread spilled through him in an icy flood. He closed the book, and when Daisy reached out her hands for it, he let her take it from him. She studied it for a few moments, clearly disappointed. 'This isn't a story book,' she said.

'No. I told you, it's history,' he murmured, his voice toneless.

'Tillie wants to know what kind of book it is,' said Daisy.

'It's... the truth,' whispered Peter. 'Simple as that.'

'Tillie says you're lying. She says it's all made up.'

'Never mind what *she* says!' snarled Peter, and was shocked by the anger in his own voice. Daisy recoiled from him and he put a hand out to reassure her. 'Sorry,' he said. 'I... I didn't mean to shout.' He looked around for something else to talk about, something to blot out the horrible thoughts that were writhing and coiling like a nest of vipers in his head. He noticed a white nightgown lying on the bed, one that he'd never seen before. 'What's this?' he asked.

Daisy looked down at it and seemed to relax a little. 'Isn't it lovely?' she said. 'It's an old one of Miss Sally's, she's too big for it now. Mrs Beesley said I could have it. I'm to wear it tonight.'

Peter nodded. He was sure now that his suspicions were right. He knew exactly what was going on here and the knowledge filled him with absolute terror. He was shaking, his whole body shuddering with the realisation of the terrible danger Daisy was in.

She was looking towards the window again.

'Yes,' she said. 'I *will*, won't I?' She smiled at Peter. 'Tillie says I'll look just like Miss Sally.'

Peter felt something click at the back of his skull. He got up from the bed and walked across to the window. He picked up the doll with his left hand and unlatched the window with his right. It might have been his imagination but he thought he felt the doll's soft body vibrating in his hand – and then there was a brief stinging sensation at the base of his index finger. He grunted and flung the doll out of the window. Then he stared at his hand. A bright trickle of crimson was pulsing from a tiny wound in the fleshy fold at the base of the finger.

'Why did you do that?' wailed Daisy. She was sitting on the bed, looking distraught.

'I didn't like her,' said Peter, closing the window and turning back to face his sister. 'I don't like dolls that talk. You shouldn't like them either.' He showed her his injured hand. 'I cut myself,' he said.

'But...now Mrs Beesley will be angry with us! She said we weren't to touch the dolls!'

'We won't tell her.' Peter paused to suck at the wound on his hand, the warm, coppery taste of his own blood filling his mouth. He sat down beside Daisy. 'I'll get you another doll,' he assured her. 'As soon as we're home.'

'It won't be able to talk like Tillie,' she told him.

'If we were home, you wouldn't *want* a doll like that,' he assured her. 'You'd see how wrong it was. It's this place. It makes bad things seem natural.' He put his right hand on her shoulder. He felt like crying but knew that he mustn't break down in front of her. He had to stay strong if they were to have any chance of survival. 'Daisy, listen to me. Tomorrow, we're leaving. You and me. We're going home.'

She brightened up at this news. 'But...we're supposed to stay here.'

'I know. That doesn't matter.'

'How...how will we get there?'

'I don't know, yet. On the train, I suppose. We'll walk if we have to. And tonight...tonight I'm going to stay here with you.'

'Why, what's wrong?' She looked worried again and he realised that his fear was infectious. He forced himself to smile.

'Nothing's wrong,' he assured her. 'I'm...looking after you, that's all. Like a brother should. Like Mum asked me to. And...it'll be fun, won't it? Just the two of us. I'll read you a bedtime story.' She nodded. He leaned closer to whisper. 'But listen, Daisy, this is really important. Don't say anything to anyone about us leaving. Do you understand? It's to be our secret. Tomorrow morning, first thing, we'll pack up our cases and we'll sneak out.'

Daisy looked excited. 'It'll be an adventure,' she said.

'Yes. An adventure. Our secret.'

He started at the sound of a knock on the door.

'Children? Your supper's ready.' Mrs Beesley's voice – cold, harsh, hateful.

'We're coming,' he called out. He looked at Daisy again. 'Remember, now. Not a word to anyone.'

Then they went downstairs for supper.

CHAPTER TWENTY

'Now,' said Mrs Beesley, smiling her phoney smile, 'how about a nice mug of hot milk before bedtime?'

Peter looked across the kitchen table at Daisy. She was nodding eagerly enough and, after a moment's thought, he agreed too. Despite everything that had happened, he found that he was ravenous. Even the generous portion of meat and mashed potatoes Mrs Beesley had given him for supper had failed to fill him up. He supposed that the long walk across the Marsh must have given him an appetite. Funny how you could be scared half out of your wits and still feel ready to eat. Night had fallen now and the wireless was once again playing a succession of syrupy dance tunes. Peter understood now why she usually had music playing at night. To drown out any other sounds the children might hear. The sound of a pipe playing out in the darkness.

There'd been no sign of Adam since they'd returned. He'd

kept himself to himself out in the stables, far from the reproachful eyes and vengeful voice of Mrs Beesley. Peter could imagine him sitting out there, sipping at his bottle of 'medicine', no doubt dreading the moment when he would have to account for his failure to keep Peter away from the Grange. Peter realised Adam was much more wary of Mrs Beesley than any curse.

Mrs Beesley had been unusually talkative over supper, as though she was trying to fill the accusing silence that hung in the room. She'd told them how she'd worked here at the Grange since she was a young girl and how Mr Sheldon had taken her in when her parents had died and she'd been left penniless. She'd told them how she owed the Sheldon family everything. She'd even mentioned the late Mrs Sheldon, what a wonderful woman she was, loved by everyone who knew her; and how tragic her death had been. Nobody could understand how a skilled young horsewoman like her could have died the way she did, her horse stumbling out on the Marsh and throwing her. The horse had come down on top of her and she'd been crushed. Peter heard the words, but there was no surprise in any of it. With everything he'd learned it seemed somehow inevitable. The Piper inflicting his long cruel vengeance on the Sheldon family.

Daisy hadn't had very much to say for herself all through the meal. She'd kept her head down, no doubt nervous about giving something away, about what had happened to Tillie or the secret plan to run away in the morning.

Now Mrs Beesley busied herself at the range, heating up a copper pan of milk. She seemed to take a very long time, hunched over two mugs. 'I'm just addin' a bit of sugar,' she told them. 'You Lunnen types likes your sugar, don't you?' She brought the steaming mugs over to the table and set them down.

Daisy gulped at her milk greedily and Peter took a small sip of his, before setting it down again.

'What's wrong with it?' asked Mrs Beesley.

'Er. . . nothing. I'm not that keen on milk, really.'

'You should have said! I could make you cocoa, if you prefer.'

'No, it's all right,' he assured her. He lifted the mug back to his lips and took another mouthful.

'It'll help you sleep,' she said, as she walked back over to the sink. 'You must be proper tired after that long walk across the Marsh. It's quite a distance, that is. That's why I told Adam to stop over in Hythe, give you a chance to rest.'

She'd obviously prepared her story while Peter was upstairs, but he didn't believe her for a moment and knew now that he wouldn't believe anything else she told him. Besides, he decided, sleep was the last thing he needed tonight. He forced down another mouthful but then, checking that her back was turned, he lifted the lid of the empty teapot on the table and quickly poured the contents of the mug into that. Daisy saw him and opened her mouth to say something, but he lifted a finger to his lips and she nodded.

Mrs Beesley filled the sink from the big kettle on the range and started washing the dishes from supper. 'So, how did you get on with Adam today?' she inquired.

'All right,' said Peter. 'We went out to Thursby Lake first. And then we went into Hythe to post the card.'

'It's a pretty town, ain't it?' said Mrs Beesley.

'Yes.' He decided to do a bit of fishing. 'Actually, when we were there, I visited the church. St Leonard's?'

'Oh,' she said. Peter noticed with a twinge of satisfaction how her shoulders stiffened at this. 'Did you now?'

'Yes. It was while Adam was in the pub.'

Now she turned and looked over her shoulder. 'I thought the two of you might stay there for the night,' she said.

'I told Adam, it would be nice for you to get away from the house for a while.'

'I wanted to come back,' he told her. 'To be with Daisy. To look after her.'

'I'm sure she's well able to look after herself,' said Mrs Beesley. She tuned away again.

Peter ignored the comment. 'It's an interesting place, St Leonard's,' he continued, studying Mrs Beesley's back as he spoke. 'The Crypt. Have you ever been down there?'

She shook her head. 'No, and you wouldn't ever catch me doing it, neither. I've heard about what's down there. Enough to give you the heebie jeebies, it is. I don't know why anybody would want to keep something like that where decent people can go and see it. In a place of worship too.'

'What's down there?' asked Daisy brightly.

'Bones,' said Peter.

'Bones?'

'Yes. You know, skeletons. There are the skulls and leg bones of thousands of people, just . . . lying around down there.'

Daisy made a face. 'That sounds horrible,' she said.

'No, it was actually jolly interesting. I spoke to the vicar. Reverend Latimer. I told him all about us and how we were staying here at the Grange.'

Now Mrs Beesley turned to look at him and Peter could see that she was far from pleased at this news. It was obvious that she'd wanted to keep the children's presence here as secret as possible. Now the news had got out and in a place like this, such news would travel fast. Perhaps, Peter thought, it was a good thing that other people knew they were here. Maybe it meant that Mrs Beesley and Mr Sheldon wouldn't dare to do anything to their visitors.

'Was he a nice vicar?' asked Daisy.

'He seemed nice enough. He told me all kinds of things about the history of the Marsh. The funny things that have gone on here. He said that—'

'Now then!' Mrs Beesley stepped suddenly away from the sink. 'I think perhaps it's time you two got yourselves off to bed.' Her tone made it clear that as far as she was concerned, the conversation was over.

'It's still quite early,' observed Peter. 'At home, we go to bed at—'

'You're not at home now!' snapped Mrs Beesley. Then she forced that phoney smile. 'Now, why don't you two go up and say goodnight to Miss Sally?' she suggested. 'But don't be keeping her for long, she needs her sleep. Lord knows, we could all do with some of that.'

There was clearly no point in trying to argue. Daisy headed for the stairs and Peter got up to follow her. As he did so, he felt a wave of tiredness sweep over him and he lifted a hand to his forehead.

'What's the matter?' asked Daisy.

'Nothing,' he muttered. But he felt decidedly odd. He gestured to her to go on and followed her up the stairs, clinging onto the bannister rail, because he was feeling slightly dizzy. On the first floor, they tapped gently on Miss Sally's door and were told to enter. There she was, sitting in bed, propped up by a stack of cushions, a book in her hands. Daisy went straight over and sat on the end of the bed, but Peter hung back, pretending to study the rows of bookshelves on one side of the room. The woozy feeling in his head was intensifying and he wondered if he was coming down with the flu.

'We came to say goodnight,' said Daisy, perching herself on the side of the bed. 'What are you reading now?'

'It's called *Secret Water*,' said Sally. 'It's the latest in the *Swallows and Amazons* series. Do you know the books?'

Daisy nodded. 'They're not really my kind of story,' she admitted. 'But Peter's read some of them, haven't you, Peter?'

Peter nodded and wished he hadn't, because it made him feel even worse. 'I've read the first three,' he said. 'I got them from the library in Dagenham. They're ... good.' He waved a hand at the bookshelves. 'What a lot of books you have,' he observed. 'There must be ... hundreds of them. I don't suppose you've got Professor Lowell's book somewhere in here?'

'The writer you met?' asked Daisy, puzzled.

'Yes.' He looked at Sally. 'I met him today when I was out with Adam. I ... I expect you know him, don't you?'

'I've met him once or twice,' admitted Sally, but her expression suggested she didn't care for him much.

'He's written a local history book, hasn't he?'

'So I believe.'

'You mean you haven't read it? I'm ... surprised. You read so many books. And this one mentions the ... the Grange.'

Sally frowned. 'Oh well, Daddy said it wasn't really for me.'

'Oh, so your father's read it?'

'Yes. When it had just been published. He said the professor had made up a lot of things.'

Peter moved closer to the bed. 'But ... why would he do that?' he asked her. 'You aren't supposed to ... to make up history, are you?'

'I don't know.' Sally shrugged dismissively. 'I prefer fiction, anyway.'

'The professor told me something interesting,' said Peter. 'He said that you...you haven't always been ill.' He sat down rather heavily at the foot of the bed and as he did so, his side bumped against Sally's feet under the covers. He felt something hard prod into him and he thought he heard the muffled clink of metal. 'He told me that...he saw you at some kind of fair in April and there was...nothing wrong with you then.'

Sally looked evasive. 'Well, yes, I suppose that's true,' she said.

'But...when I talked to your father, he said you've... always been weak...I thought that meant you've been like this for a long time.' Peter lifted a hand to his head again. It was throbbing now. He felt like he needed some air.

'Well, I suppose he just meant that I get colds and so forth. That's all.'

'So when...when did you first find that you...couldn't get out of bed?'

Sally looked flustered. 'It...it's not that I *can't*. It's just that I'm not allowed to. Especially not at night. Daddy says...he says it's too dangerous...'

'I...I'm only...' Peter swayed to one side and put out a hand to stop himself from falling. His fingers touched something hard beneath the bed covers and once again, there was that tell-tale clink of metal. He stared down at the bed for a moment. A sudden conviction had come over him. His head was buzzing and the room seemed to be swaying giddily around him. 'What...what's under there?' he murmured, pointing to the foot of the bed.

'Nothing,' insisted Sally, but her face told him she was lying.

Summoning his last reserves of strength, Peter stood up. He reached out a hand and took hold of the covers at the foot of the bed.

'Don't!' cried Sally. 'You're not supposed—'

Peter yanked the covers roughly aside, exposing Sally's bare feet. He stared down in horrified amazement. Her ankles were clamped by a pair of stout metal shackles. From them, a short length of chain ran to the metal frame of the bed. Peter recoiled and stood there, swaying, staring down at her feet. Daisy was staring too, her mouth open.

'Daddy says it's for the best!' cried Sally. 'They put them on me every night. It's to stop me from sleepwalking.'

'Sleepwalking?' murmured Peter. 'Or dancing?'

Sally's eyes filled with tears. 'I can still hear the music,' she said. 'Even with the earplugs in, I can hear it. It calls to me. And I . . . I want to go out and dance with the other girls. But Daddy says I can't go. I've begged him to let me, but he won't. And I want to. I want to so badly!'

And then Peter remembered something he'd heard a couple of times, late at night when he was drifting off to sleep. The sound of metal clinking against metal. And he knew what it was now. Sally, trying to get free of the chains, so she could go out and join the girls waiting for her in the mist-shrouded garden.

Peter tried to say something else but words failed him. He could only dumbly point at her shackled feet. He was aware that Daisy was looking up at him now and asking him what was wrong, but her voice seemed to boom and echo meaninglessly. The room had turned into a crazy carnival ride, a blur of garish colours that whirled and swayed around his head.

He was dimly aware of the bedroom door opening and somebody coming into the room. Then hands were closing around him, lifting him up off the ground and he tried to struggle, but his limbs had turned to mush and a heavy blackness was pushing into his head, swallowing everything. He went down into the darkness and knew no more.

PART THREE

FINALE

CHAPTER TWENTY-ONE

Grandad Peter stops talking again. Helen stares at him.

'She...she drugged you?' she gasps. 'That Mrs Beesley. She gave you something to make you sleep?'

Grandad Peter nods. 'She wanted to be certain that I wouldn't wake up that night,' he says, as though that explains everything.

'That...that horrible woman! How...how could she do such a thing to a...a boy?'

Grandad Peter sighs. He turns his head and looks out of the window at the rain-lashed garden and the skeletal branches swaying in the wind. 'I've had a lot of time to think about Mrs Beesley,' he tells her. 'In the end, I decided that she was acting out of love.'

'Love?' Helen stares at him.

'Yes. Love for Sally and dedication to Mr Sheldon. Sometimes, people can persuade themselves to do the most *unimaginable things in the name of love. The most wicked, hurtful things. I didn't see it then, I was too young to understand. It's only in the fullness of time that you come to realise the full extent of what people are really capable of.' He frowned and sighed. 'I still don't know what it was she put in that milk,' he said. 'Only that it was very powerful. And if I'd taken one mouthful more of it, we probably wouldn't be having this conversation now.'*

Helen looks at him. It is suddenly very quiet in the room. She is aware of the beating of her own heart within her chest, as Grandad Peter continues with his story.

CHAPTER TWENTY-TWO

Images swam around in Peter's head like the contents of a nightmarish aquarium. Mysterious shadowy pipers pursued children across midnight marshes. Hideous faces floated to the surface of pools of stagnant water and grimaced at him. Sheep bleated, birds flapped and a wolf loped silently along the bank of a canal. Through it all ran that music, high and keening, seeming to fill his head with its lilting tones.

And then quite suddenly, he was awake, lying on his bed in the attic. It took him a little while to come back to his senses, to realise that he was fully clothed and stretched out on the covers. His mouth was parched, his head throbbed and above all else, that infernal flute music rose and fell. At first he thought it was simply in his head, but then he realised that it was actually coming from somewhere outside the house. He tried to remember what had happened earlier, but for a moment his thoughts were insubstantial wisps of cloud, floating this way and that, eluding him completely.

Then everything swam abruptly back into focus. He sat up on the bed and gasped. He'd been drugged, he was in no doubt about that – but he hadn't drunk much of the milk and that must have been what had saved him. He swung his legs around onto the floor and got himself upright, but for the moment, his limbs felt rubbery and out of control. He stumbled across to the nightstand, picked up the big jug of water and raising it to his mouth, took a long noisy swig from its contents, sloshing half of it down the front of his shirt. He poured more into the basin, set the jug down and scooped the water onto his face, its coldness making him gasp. He stood there trying to pull himself together.

A vision rose in his head, the image of his sister's face, an expression of terror etched into every feature. He groaned and lurched around towards the door of his room, telling himself he had to go to her before it was too late. He wrenched open the door and went outside. He stood at the top of the first flight of stairs, listening. Outside, the music was still playing, the same simple refrain he had heard the previous night, repeating itself over and over. He listened for a moment, his blood seeming to chill in his veins.

'Daisy!' he gasped. He went down the stairs to her room and pushed open the door. Moonlight was flooding in through the window and he saw in an instant that her bed was empty, the covers strewn in an untidy heap on the floor. Now fear spilled through him, as sharp and cold as a knife blade. He crossed the room and went to the window to look out. As ever, that infernal mist hung low to the ground. He saw nothing in the garden itself, but when he lifted his gaze to the avenue of trees that led out to the gates, he caught sight of several figures moving through the mist, making it writhe and coil around them. Most of them were too far away to see clearly but the nearest of them was Daisy, he was sure of that. She was dressed in the white nightgown that Mrs Beesley had given to her and she was following the other figures, who seemed to be dancing along through the gates of the house, but for the moment he paid them no attention. If he could just get to Daisy in time...

He backed away from the window and then noticed one other detail. A row of dolls sat on the window seat, smiling up at him. Among them sat Tillie, her white teeth bared in what looked like a grin of triumph. Tillie. But how had she got back inside? He snatched up the doll, threw her to the ground and brought down his heel hard on that grinning face, smashing it to fragments. Then he turned and ran out of the room and along the corridor. As he passed Sally's door, he heard sounds from within, the clanking of a metal chain, the furious gasping of breath as she struggled to free herself but there was no time to think about that now. He went down the next flight of stairs. He'd intended to go straight out of the front door, but he came to an abrupt halt halfway down the stairs when he saw that somebody was sitting on a wooden chair in front of the door. Mrs Beesley. She had been dozing, her head tilted forward, but Peter's footsteps must have woken her. She lifted her head and her eyes opened. She stared up at him in silence, her expression furious.

'I *knew* you hadn't drunk it all,' she growled.

He took another step down. 'You...you have to let me go,' he told her. 'Daisy's out there.' He pointed towards the door. 'I...I saw her from the window.'

'Go back to bed, boy,' she said, and her voice was expressionless. 'You've been dreaming, that's all.'

'No.' He shook his head. 'No, Daisy's not in her room. I saw her in the garden. You must let me out.'

'Why didn't you stay overnight in Hythe?' she asked him, shaking her head. 'It would have been so much easier if you had.'

'You must let me help her,' pleaded Peter. 'She's with other people out there. Strangers. Something terrible could happen to her.'

He heard footsteps coming from the direction of the sitting room and Mr Sheldon came slowly along the hallway. 'Do what you're told, boy,' he said gruffly. 'Go back to bed.' His voice was badly slurred and his face was red, as though he'd been drinking heavily.

'But my sister's out there,' pleaded Peter, pointing again. 'She's in danger. Please, she's just a little girl, you have to let me go to her.'

Mr Sheldon shook his head. 'Best you stay away,' he said. 'There's nothing you can do for her now.'

Peter stared at him in desperation. 'Please,' he whispered. 'I . . . I promised our mother that I would look after her.'

But Mr Sheldon didn't seem to be listening. He was gazing towards the door as though he could somehow see beyond it. 'You think I'm proud of this?' he murmured. 'You think I like what I've had to do? I lost my wife years ago and Sally is all I have left in the world. Don't you see, boy, I couldn't lose her too? I just *couldn't*. To prevent that, I'm prepared to pay any price.'

Peter licked his lips. He was aware that as he stood here

talking, Daisy was getting further and further away from the house. Who knew what might happen to her out in the darkness? Meanwhile, Mr Sheldon went right on talking. 'I didn't believe it,' he said. 'I really didn't. Superstitious mumbo-jumbo, I told them, nothing more! That's what I believed back then. Of course, I...I knew about the earlier deaths, but I put them down to coincidence and exaggeration. I told myself, this is the twentieth century, such things cannot happen now. I truly believed that! Even when my wife died in such a terrible way, I dismissed it as bad luck. I really thought Sally would be safe here...and then...then she started hearing the music.' A look of cold dread came to his eyes. 'At first, I put it down to fanciful imagination. You see, I have never heard it, not once. Mrs Beesley has heard nothing, Adam has heard nothing. What about you boy? I expect you can hear it, can't you?'

Peter nodded, licked his dry lips. 'It's like a flute playing,' he said. 'It's louder every night. But listen, while we stand here talking...'

'Something to do with age, I suppose. Only the children can hear it. I was adamant that such a thing could not be, but when Sally told me that even with the earplugs in, she could *still* hear it, it began to dawn on me that there really was something evil at work here, something that has been returning to this area over the years. Something malevolent.' He shook his head, as though trying to rid himself of the idea. 'And then I read how after you start hearing the music, he comes for you on a certain date. The seventh. Always the seventh. That's when he's at his most powerful. Some children manage to hang on for a day or so, but the music calls to them and in the end, they have to give in to it. And they say it doesn't matter where you go, you can't hide. One of my ancestors went to live in London, but his youngest child drowned, just like the rest of 'em.'

'Please!' cried Peter. 'Let me out. My sister…'

But Mr Sheldon didn't seem to be listening. He was confessing…but whether to Peter or to some higher authority, it was impossible to say.

'And then it occurred to me. A possible answer to my problems. The Piper always demands his fee. Why not give him what he wants and let him go on his way again?' He smiled, shook his head. 'He demands a life. A young girl's life, the price for being murdered by my ancestors. Oh yes, that's clearly what happened. Not any of my doing, but my penance just the same. The sins of the fathers are visited on the children. Isn't that what they say?'

'Mr Sheldon,' said Mrs Beesley. 'The boy doesn't have to hear everything.'

'But why not?' snarled Mr Sheldon. 'He knows too much already, why not tell him the rest? We can't allow him to leave and talk to others about what's happened here. Perhaps if he'd stayed away as we planned . . .' He shook his head. 'Now, I fear, he knows too much. He's a loose end. So why not let him hear everything before we . . . tie it?'

Peter shook his head, tears in his eyes now. 'My sister,' he whispered. 'She's out there on her own.'

Mr Sheldon shook his head and chuckled horribly. 'Not on her own, boy. If only it were so. If only life were that kind.'

Peter licked his lips and looked desperately around the hallway. Mrs Beesley had risen from her chair and was standing in front of the doorway. Mr Sheldon was leaning against the wall just along the hallway to his left. On a small table, a paraffin lamp lit the scene with a harsh, yellow light.

'Then I heard about the evacuees,' said Mr Sheldon, gazing up at Peter. 'Displaced, needing somewhere to stay. I thought to myself, well, why not offer somebody else in my daughter's place? It's always a girl he takes. I don't know why that should be the case, but I saw that perhaps I could turn it to my advantage. Perhaps the Piper could be tricked. He demands a life, how is he to know if he has the right person? I don't know if it will work, but I have to try something. And tonight is the night he's at his most powerful. Sally is so desperate to go out there. I had to stop her somehow...'

'By keeping her chained up?' Peter gazed down at the man in disgust.

'I didn't know what else to do! Don't you understand, that girl is all I have in the world? There's no price too severe that I wouldn't pay it, even if it means that I'm damned to eternal torment because of it. And I *am* damned. I know that. I know that only too well.' Mr Sheldon began to sob. He lifted his hands to his face and covered his eyes.

Peter saw his opportunity. He looked down into the hallway and gauged the distance, knowing that he had to act now, that he couldn't afford to wait a moment longer. He snatched in a breath, put one hand on the rail and vaulted nimbly over the bannister. He came down awkwardly between the two adults and threw out an arm to steady himself. His hand inadvertently caught the edge of the hall table and overturned it, knocking over the paraffin lamp, but there was no time to hesitate because Mr Sheldon was lunging at him, arms outstretched to grab him by the throat. Peter ducked under his grasp and in the same instant, there was a fierce *whoosh* as the lamp hit the ground by Mrs Beesley's feet and exploded into flame. The hem of her long dress caught alight and then she screamed as a sudden burst of fire engulfed her.

Peter ran along the hallway and into the nearest room, aware as he did so that Mr Sheldon was running towards Mrs Beesley, removing his coat as he went, meaning to use it in an attempt to staunch the flames that had engulfed her. Her agonised screams rent the air.

Peter didn't hesitate. He found himself in what looked like a study. He approached the big bow window and reached up to try and unlatch it, but the handle wouldn't open and he suspected it was locked shut. He looked desperately around, spotted a heavy mahogany stool in one corner and went to pick it up. Then he spun round, ran back to the window and, lifting one arm to cover his face, threw the stool with all his strength at the leaded glass. There was an abrupt shattering sound as it smashed through. Peter ran to the window, started pushing out the jagged edges of the glass and then, deciding that he couldn't waste any more time, began to clamber through the opening.

He was halfway out when a hand grabbed his shoulder and started to wrench him back. He turned his head and saw Mr Sheldon's soot-blackened face, inches from his, his eyes bulging, his expression manic. 'Not so fast, boy,' he growled, but Peter was intent only on getting out of the house and going to his sister's aid. He yanked up an arm and elbowed Mr Sheldon hard in the face. He heard a grunt of surprise, felt Sheldon's nose flatten under the impact and the man's fingers loosened their grip. Peter pulled free and scrambled through the opening, tearing the leg of his trousers on a jagged piece of glass as he went. He was blind to everything now but his need to get to Daisy. He dropped to the ground and crouched for a moment, catching his breath. Then he straightened up and began to run round the side of the house, aware as he did so of the thick pall of black smoke that was gushing out from around the closed front door.

There was no time to hesitate. He had to get to Daisy. He had to get to her before it was too late, and who knew how far she'd gone by now? He knew only too well where she'd be headed. He put his head down and ran as fast as his legs could carry him.

CHAPTER TWENTY-THREE

Peter pounded down the driveway towards the open gate. He threw a look back over his shoulder and saw to his dismay that the fire seemed to have taken hold in the house. Through a couple of ground-floor windows, he could see the restless orange glare of the flames. He hesitated, wondering if he should go back to help, but then told himself that whatever happened in there, Mr Sheldon had brought it upon himself. Peter could not be held responsible. And he had lost too much time already.

He went through the gate and paused for a moment, listening intently. He couldn't see Daisy or the ghost children. The music was louder out here and it seemed to his confused senses to be coming from somewhere off to his right, so he ignored the road ahead of him and turned onto the Marsh, following the track where Adam had taken him earlier that same day. He ran in silence, his head down, the cold air reviving his muddled thoughts. The music grew steadily louder as he ran.

After a little distance, he became dimly aware of the line of trees off to his left, indicating the long run of the Military Canal. He continued to run alongside it for quite a distance, straining to see through the misty darkness. He seemed to run for an age before he thought he spotted a glimpse of movement under the trees by the near bank. He slowed his pace, turned off the path and headed cautiously towards it. As he drew steadily closer, a ray of moonlight breaking through the cloud cover revealed a number of girls standing beneath the shadows of the trees. No, not standing, he decided, moving. Dancing. Swaying to the music, just as the girls had danced the other night. There were five of them in all and he knew who they were. The Piper's drowned victims, brought back to welcome a new member to their ranks. In their midst, he could see a familiar figure, a little girl with blonde hair, dressed in a white nightgown. She was dancing inexpertly with the others, flailing her arms, stamping her bare feet. Peter's heart thudded in his chest as he registered that it was Daisy. But even as he recognised her, the music fell suddenly silent and the children stopped dancing. They turned threateningly towards Daisy and began to close in on her. She looked around at them, as though coming out of a trance. She gave a gasp of terror.

'No!' Peter started to run again, covering the distance as fast as he could, pumping his arms and stretching out his legs. He could see that Daisy was backing away from the other children, backing slowly towards the edge of the canal. Peter remembered with a sudden shrill of pure dread that she had never learned to swim. And then a thought occurred to him. Five girls... but shouldn't there be six of them? He was closer now. If he could just get to her in time...

He was only yards away when he saw that something was rising up from the water behind Daisy – a pair of long skeletal arms. The sixth girl. He stared in horror as two filthy green hands clamped suddenly around Daisy's ankles and dragged her backwards into the water.

Peter screamed in absolute terror and some of the girls turned their heads to look in his direction. He recognised the closest of them. She had the face that he kept seeing in his nightmares, but he steeled himself and kept running straight at her. As he crashed into her, the girl's body seemed to disappear in a cloud of dust. Another girl lunged towards him and he swung an arm at her, making her, too, vanish in an instant. Then he was running on towards the edge of the canal. He saw something moving in the dark water, caught a glimpse of Daisy's white nightgown, around which two dark arms were clamped. There was a flash of blonde hair, Daisy's frantic eyes staring up at him and then she was dragged down beneath the surface, her arms flailing, her legs kicking.

Peter didn't hesitate. He threw himself headlong into the canal and dived beneath the surface, the icy water filling his eyes and chilling him to the bone. He threw out his hands in the direction where Daisy had sunk and, for a moment, his fingers encountered sodden fabric, but then it was wrenched abruptly from his grasp and something wet and slimy clamped around his own wrist. His heart hammered in his chest and he struggled to escape, opening his mouth to cry out, swallowing mouthfuls of foul-tasting water. He kicked himself free and struggled back to the surface, coughing and spluttering. He snatched in another breath and dived again, kicking his legs to try and push himself down as far as he could, struggling to keep his eyes open so he could peer into the murky depths, but the canal seemed to be bottomless and he had to power his way down for what seemed an age, before he finally saw something.

He caught a glimpse of Daisy's white face, gazing imploringly up at him, her arms outstretched towards him and he tried desperately to get to her, struggling with every ounce of strength left in his body, but something had her gripped around the waist, some hideous, rotting thing that was far more powerful than she. There was a last swirl and then Daisy and her captor were gone and Peter, his air exhausted, was obliged to kick his way to the surface again, gasping for breath. He broke water, sobbing, and looked frantically around the canal bank, thinking of shouting for help. But for the moment, there was only one solitary figure moving away along the bank, his pipe slung across his shoulder.

'Wait!' screamed Peter. 'Please. You've got the wrong person. Come back!'

The Piper paused and glanced back over his shoulder. In the moonlight, Peter caught a glimpse of his face. It was little more than a skull, flecked here and there with scraps of shrivelled flesh. From the deep eye sockets a pair of fathomless red eyes glared at him. Cold, merciless, they showed no shred of pity. Then, in the near distance, there was a sudden blaze of light as the fire finally burst through the thatched roof of the Grange. The Piper turned to look for a moment. Then figures began to materialise behind him, one by one – the ragged girls, following him once again as he strode away – but now there were seven of them. The last figure in the procession looked strangely familiar. She paused for a moment and glanced back over her shoulder. Peter caught a shocking glimpse of a hideously burned face and twists of melted red hair, stuck to the creature's head. He gasped as he recognised her and shouted her name.

Sally didn't react. She turned her ruined face away and followed the others. After a few moments, the procession faded into the shadows of the trees. Peter was left alone, thrashing in the water... but a sudden rush of new hope was rising within him.

He snatched in a deep breath and dived again, powering himself down, down into the depths, his questing hands desperately groping for whatever they could find, discovering nothing but fronds of slimy green weed and broken branches that had fallen from the trees. He stayed down there until his lungs ached and his head swam and he was about to admit defeat, when the fingers of his right hand closed around something soft and firm, hidden amongst a tangle of weeds. A wrist. He pulled hard and something shifted in the water and bumped against him. He threw his arms around whatever it was and kicked his way upwards, dragging the weight along with him. He broke the surface, gasping for air. Now he could see what he held in his arms. It was Daisy, but her eyes were closed, her face pale and lifeless. Near exhaustion, he swam to the bank, pulling her clumsily after him and somehow, he got her up out of the water and onto the grass. He clambered out and kneeled beside her, staring desperately at her white face.

'Daisy!' he gasped. 'Daisy, wake up!'

There was no reaction. Her eyes were closed, her mouth open. Beneath the sodden nightgown, her chest was still. He didn't know what to do and for a moment he was frozen, defeated. But then he willed himself to take control. He placed his hands on her chest and pushed hard. A pulse of brown water pumped from her mouth, so he tried again, with the same result. Her eyes remained closed. He looked up at the indifferent stars above him.

'Please!' he cried, but he didn't know who or what he was shouting to. He studied Daisy for a moment more, then lifted a fist and brought it down hard on her chest and this time, she sat up with a loud cough and threw up more water. 'Ow!' she rasped, staring at him blankly. 'That hurt!'

'Daisy!' he gasped. 'Oh, Daisy…' He put his arms around her and pulled her to him, crying tears of relief.

'Was I dreaming?' she whispered, beside his ear.

'Yes,' he told her. 'A very bad dream. But you're awake now.'

'Then why are you crying?' she asked him. He didn't know what to tell her, so he just hugged her tight and told her that everything would be all right.

When he looked up again, he saw that now a great fire was burning at the Grange, blazing up through its collapsed roof, a fire that must have been visible for miles. And next, he heard a sound, the juddering, rattling sound of a cart approaching at speed. He made out a dark shape lurching towards him across the uneven ground and, after a few moments, he could discern the hulking figure of Adam, hunched behind the reins. Adam pulled Bessie to a halt and jumped to the ground. He ran over and threw himself to his knees beside Peter, his eyes wide and staring.

'The house,' he gasped and Peter saw that he was crying like a child. 'It's all gone. I tried to help, but the flames... they beat me back. They're gone too. Mr Sheldon, Mrs B... and Sally. Poor Sally. All gone.' He looked at the figure that was cradled in Peter's arms. 'Miss Daisy?' he whispered fearfully.

'She's all right,' Peter assured him. 'I thought I'd lost her, but I...I got her back again.' He pointed into the trees. 'I saw him, Adam. The Piper. Sally was with him...'

Adam stared at him for several moments, not understanding. 'No,' he said, at last. 'No, no, that's not... possible.'

'I saw her,' Peter said again. 'He took Sally with him.'

Adam shook his head and his eyes filled with fresh tears.

'I...I didn't really believe,' he said. 'I thought they'd all gone mad. I never really believed anything would 'appen.' I never...' He stared helplessly at Peter, a look of anguish on his face. 'And now it's all gone. The Grange...everything.' He got to his feet and helped Peter up. He stooped and picked up Daisy, who lay in his arms staring around as though she didn't have the first idea where she was or how she had got here. Adam carried her to the cart and set her up in the seat, where she sat slumped and bewildered. Peter scrambled up beside her, while Adam ran round to the back and got the blanket. He climbed up beside them and draped the blanket around them both. Peter put an arm around his sister's shoulders and she snuggled against him in stunned silence. She was shivering now.

'Where are we going?' whispered Peter.

'To Hythe,' said Adam. 'I'll drop you at the police station.'

'And...you? You'll stay with us?'

Adam shook his head. 'I can't,' he said. 'I'll have to leave you there.'

'But...where will you go?'

Adam shrugged his shoulders. 'The Lookers' huts,' he said. 'I know where all of them are. If I stay on the move, they won't find me.'

'But...you've done nothing wrong. Why...?'

'There'll be questions,' Adam told him. 'Questions I'll never be able to answer in a hundred years.' He placed a hand on Peter's shoulder. 'Please don't tell them where to look for me.'

They stared at each other in silence for a moment. Then Peter nodded. Adam cracked the whip, urged Bessie round in a wide circle, and headed back towards the road. They galloped into Hythe in the moonlight, neither of them saying a word to each other, until finally, Adam dropped Peter and Daisy outside a brick building with a blue lamp burning outside it. He looked down at them for a moment and said, 'I never believed. Not for one moment. If I had, I'd never have gone along with them. You know that, don't you?'

Peter nodded. 'I believe you,' he said.

'Keep safe,' whispered Adam. He snapped the whip again and the cart clattered away. Peter watched as it vanished into the darkness. He stood where he was for a moment, holding tightly onto Daisy. Then he led her across the road to the blue lamp.

By then, she was almost catatonic, and he wasn't much better. The police carried Daisy to a bunk in an empty cell, where they got her dry and wrapped her in blankets. She fell instantly into a deep sleep. Then they made Peter a cup of hot, sweet tea and asked him questions about what had happened out at the Grange, what he had seen out there. He could only stare at them in silence. He didn't speak to a soul, not until they'd driven him and Daisy back to Dagenham and they were safely back in their mother's house. It was only when he saw Daisy smile for the first time in days, that he knew it was really over and he could finally relax.

Then he went up to his room and slept for two whole days.

CHAPTER TWENTY-FOUR

The silence in Grandad Peter's room is oppressive. They sit there, looking at the window and the gloomy garden outside. For a long time, they don't say anything.

'I had no idea,' says Helen at last. She's aware that her eyes are full of tears. Grandad Peter is sitting beside her, looking at his hands, as though trying to puzzle them out.

'Why would you?' he murmurs. 'I've never really spoken of it since it happened. And if I had, what would people have thought? That I was mad, no doubt. That I needed to be locked away for my own safety, and the safety of others.' He shakes his head. 'They all died in the fire. Sheldon, Mrs Beesley, poor Sally. When I think of her, chained to the bed in that room as it filled with smoke...' He closes his eyes for a moment as if to try and dispel the image, then opens them again. 'A fire that I started,' he adds. 'It burned so fiercely there was hardly anything left of their bodies. As for

Adam, I don't know what happened to him, I never saw nor heard from him again. I told everyone that Daisy and I had been out of the house when the fire started. That I didn't know how it was caused.'

Helen frowns. 'And no questions were asked?'

Grandad Peter shrugs. 'There was a war on. Things tended to get overlooked in those troubled times. People had bigger fish to fry. I imagine the only man with any idea of what really happened was Professor Lowell, but he was already an old man when I met him and I believe he died only a few months later. You know, I actually tried to find a copy of his book a few years back, but I had no luck with that, even using the Internet. Like so many other things connected to the story, it has disappeared without trace. Swept under the carpet. As far as I'm aware there have been no more female heirs to the Sheldon family. The bloodline stopped right there when the Grange burned down. But…' He looks troubled. 'Sometimes I can't help but ask myself. What if the curse somehow transferred itself to us? Through Daisy, I mean. After all, she cheated the Piper.'

'Daisy,' murmurs Helen. 'How come I've never heard of her?'

'*She stopped using that name soon afterwards,*' says Grandad Peter. '*Thought it was too childish, I suppose. I dare say that you've heard of Aunt Margaret, though.*'

Helen stares at him. '*What, Auntie Margaret from Australia?*'

He smiles. '*Yes. She emigrated out there when she was nineteen. Met a young army chap and married him. You remember she used to send you presents every Christmas, when you were little? Boomerangs... toy koala bears...*'

Helen nods. '*I've still got them somewhere. In a box in the attic. I never met her. I think Dad has some photos of her, though. We were always talking about going over there to visit but... I suppose we just never got around to it. And she never came back to England?*'

'*No. She was... a bit of a loner. Her husband died young and she... well, she preferred her own company.*' He smiles, ruefully. '*Remind you of anyone?*'

Helen nods. '*I suppose so.*'

'*I think what happened to us out on the Marsh made us that way. Mistrustful of strangers. Slow to make friends.*'

Helen looks worried. '*And... she died, didn't she? Quite a long time ago, I think. I was still only little when it happened.*'

Grandad Peter nods. 'Oh yes. It was some years back. But she died of natural causes. Nothing sinister. There was talk about some of us going out to the funeral but...it stayed talk.'

'That's terrible,' says Helen. 'Somebody should have gone.'

'I expect you're right. But it was hardly convenient. She didn't even live in a city. Preferred a little place in the Outback. We used to exchange letters now and then. And I spoke to her on the phone, once or twice, though it cost a fortune. She never wanted to talk about what happened to us on the Marsh. I brought it up once but she changed the subject. That was the last time we spoke, I think.'

'But...to be forgotten like that.'

'She's not forgotten,' says Grandad Peter. 'She's with me every day.'

Helen gazes at him for a moment, then thinks she understands. 'Well, I...suppose memories are like that, aren't they? They stay with you.' She thinks for a moment. 'Does Dad know? About what happened to you on the Marsh?'

'I never told him any of it. I suppose I didn't want to burden him. I'm already beginning to regret telling you.'

'Oh no, please don't feel bad. I'm...glad that you told me. It makes me feel...special.'

He forces a thin smile. 'Just the same, I think it's best if the story goes no further,' he says. 'It'll be our secret, if you don't mind. I'd prefer that.'

'All right,' she says. 'Whatever you think.'

He sighs, looks at her.

'So,' he says. 'Now you know everything that happened on the Marsh. Still interested in doing that school trip?'

Helen looks at him. 'I...I don't suppose it would be the same area or anything,' she says. 'I'm not a Sheldon, either. And I'm older than eight. So...what are the chances?'

There's a short silence. 'I wouldn't like to estimate them,' he says. 'But I'd be worried to death every day that you were there.'

She considers for a moment. 'I think I'll be taking my name off the list,' she says.

She glances at her watch and is momentarily surprised to see how late it is. 'Whoa! I need to get going! Dad will be wondering what's happened to me.' She gets up from the rocking chair, reaches for her jacket and slips it on. Then she walks across to Grandad Peter, leans over and

*pecks him on the cheek. 'You take good care of yourself,'
she tells him. 'I'll come and see you again, soon.'*

He looks up at her and his expression is as grim as ever.

'Next birthday, perhaps?' he says.

*'Don't be silly,' she says. 'Sooner than that. Next
week.'*

'Don't feel you have to,' he tells her.

*'I want to,' she assures him. She reaches out and squeezes
his hand, then buttons her jacket. 'And ... happy birthday,'
she says, but under the circumstances, it seems an incredibly
inappropriate thing to say.*

'Take care on that bicycle,' he warns her.

*She gives him a last smile, slings the empty rucksack over
her shoulder and goes out of the room, closing the door
gently behind her.*

*Grandad Peter sits there for a long time, gazing out of the
window. The wind is getting worse out there, bending the
branches of the trees.*

'Did I do the right thing?' he asks at last.

A pause.

*'It just seemed like the best thing to do, that's all. She
needed to know and I needed to talk about it.'*

Another pause.

'Yes, Daisy, it is a lovely cake, isn't it? Perhaps we'll have a slice of it with a cup of tea, later.'

Pause.

He smiles fondly. 'Well, you would say that, wouldn't you?'

Beside him, the empty rocking chair begins to move.

AFTERWORD

Most of the elements in this story have been invented . . . but not all of them.

Operation Pied Piper really happened. Thousands of children from the major cities of the British Isles were sent out to stay in the countryside with people they didn't know. You can read some of their true accounts here:

www.bbc.co.uk/history/british/britain_wwtwo/ evacuccs_01.shtml

Sheldon Grange and its inhabitants are fictitious.

The Royal Military Canal really exists – and large sections of it were dug by French prisoners of war. You can read about it here:

www.royalmilitarycanal.com/pages/index.asp

So far as I'm aware, Captain Micheaux did not exist. **The Church of St Leonard's** in Hythe is also genuine – and you can visit its Crypt where there really are the thigh bones and skulls of thousands of unidentified people. You can read about it here:

www.stleonardschurchhythekent.org

But don't waste too much time looking for an inscription in French...

NIGHT ON TERROR ISLAND

PHILIP CAVENEY

It's the scariest movie ever and they're stuck in it!

Have you ever wanted to be in the movies? Kip has, and when he meets mysterious Mr Lazarus he thinks his dream's come true because Mr Lazarus can project people into movies. Films like Terror Island, full of hungry sabre-toothed tigers and killer Neanderthals.

When Kip's in a film, everything is real: real bullets, real swords, real monsters. But he must

beware . . . if he doesn't get out by the time the closing credits roll, he'll be trapped in the film forever! Can Kip rescue his sister before the sabre-toothed tigers get her? And if he can – how is he going to get back?!

9781849392709 £6.99

HAUNTED

**A FANTASTIC COLLECTION OF GHOST STORIES
FROM TODAY'S LEADING CHILDREN'S AUTHORS**

'A chilling slice of horror. An excellent balance of
traditional and modern and a perfect pocket-money
purchase for winter evenings.' *Daily Mail*

Derek Landy, Philip Reeve, Joseph Delaney, Susan
Cooper, Eleanor Updale, Jamila Gavin, Mal Peet, Matt
Haig, Berlie Doherty, Robin Jarvis and Sam Llewellyn
have come together to bring you eleven ghost stories:
from a ghost walk around York; to a drowned boy,
who's determined to find someone to play with; to a
lost child trapped in a mirror, ready
to pull you in; to devilish creatures,
waiting with bated breath for their
next young victim; to an ancient
woodland reawakened. Some will
make you scream, some will make
you shiver, but all will haunt you
gently long after you've put the
book down.

9781849393218 £6.99